Sweet Like Saltwater

Stories

Raywat Deonandan

Intanjible Publishing

Original edition published by TSAR Publications in 1999

Republished by Intanjible Publications in 2015

www.intanjible.com

As with everything else in my life, the strength and inspiration required to complete this collection flowed from the two people who have never disappointed me, and to whom some of these stories truly belong: my parents, Sursati and Walter Deonandan.

Contents

Introduction

THE RELATIONSHIP between the peoples of India and their English conquerors is sometimes characterized as a partnership, an amicable exercise of political and social design that has resulted in the transplantation of Indian societies to all earthly domains pacified by British military might. The flourishing homogenous Indian communities in Malaysia, Singapore, Mauritius, East Africa, and, later, North America are offered as the outcomes of such a "partnership." In truth, of course, the design was entirely one-sided: a conscious attempt to impose a ready-made Indian middle class to provide a buffer between the conquering rulers and the angry masses of the ruled.

Thus was the founding and the administration of a global empire made far simpler by the provision of an unconsciously cooperative race of brown-skinned merchants, bureaucrats, farmers and intellectuals. The nature of imperialism is such that, in the final analysis, all conquered peoples become base and purposeful human capital.

Nearly two hundred years ago, indentured servants were brought to the Caribbean from places scattered throughout the British empire. Among them were my ancestors who chose the terrors and hazards of hard labour and sea voyage rather than face a horrible famine in their mother country, India. Betrayed by their overlords, who refused them their promised passage home, these men and women resignedly carved out unique societies in Guyana, Trinidad and Jamaica, desperately attempting to recreate the ancientness and familiarity of their South Asian motherland.

Though their descendants would call themselves *Indian*, they would be in essence something new, both exciting and somewhat sad: cultural hybrids of Indian, British, Portuguese, African and Chinese influences, grasping for stronger connections to the homogeneous societies left generations in the past.

We *grasp* in the food we eat, the tales we tell, and the dreams we concoct in uneasy slumber. In these ways we contemplate the Indian*ness* of our new societies, enhanced by remembered Indian words, fables and songs, reinforced by a few Indian foods that were spiced by the conflict and desires introduced by alien fraternal races, and lovingly corrupted by the inescapable caresses of the warm Caribbean ocean.

When my family moved to Canada, the grasping continued, spurred further by the daily reminder of one's own foreign nature, and necessitated by the realization that a reconciliation must be made between one's chosen home and the ancestral memories that scream from within the veins. The memories of blood extrude into one's nightly dreams and waking desires, forcing a reckoning of racial identity with cultural history and with the uncertainty of every step taken in a life that spans continents. I wonder, sometimes, if dreamers in those other pockets of transposed cross-culturization Malaysia, Singapore and Africa are also visited by messengers from deep within ancestral memory.

The history of a people can indeed be imprinted into its children's blood, to be tasted by the subconscious in times of introspection, love and candour. And for we displaced Indian children of the Caribbean, as distant as our birth from that realm may seem, the taste of our blood's history is as sweet as the saltwater of that warm sea.

Children of the Melange

I WASN'T there, but from the many subsequent retellings, I can now see it vividly when Millie's reckless boy Ravi found the corked bottle by the sea wall.

They say it glowed green like poison algae, or black like the Caribbean night sky. It bobbed along, seemingly tossed by the random ocean waves, but we all know it was guided to a specific place and time.

There are probably hundreds of such bottles, some older even than the little nations they orbit. In them, sometimes, are sealed the hopes of a family, letters to a lover, a drop of blood squeezed from a choking heart, and sometimes the shadows of wandering souls and lost travellers.

So when young Ravi stupidly uncorked the bottle, no one was truly surprised that he was taken by the ghost of the Dutchman.

His hard brown body had quaked, then stiffened, bathed in the salty sea air that is now so missed by we expatriates. From the fissure of his cracked and trembling lips had slipped mystic gurglings and senseless vociferations, gibberish to the watching few.

If it were not for Lal Bharat, himself a wanderer from neighbouring Surinam, no one would have known that Ravi was actually pronouncing fluent archaic Dutch.

Lal Bharat had held him down on his knees while Long Baba, the old village India-man, grasped a handful of hair from the crown of Ravi's head.

"Loose me! Let me go!" Ravi had pleaded, in Dutch, English, Creole and, some observers of unquestionable candour had sworn, ancient Babylonian. Instead, Long Baba had torn those hairs from Ravi's scalp, stuffed them back into the wretched bottle, recorked it, and tossed it back into the embracing sea.

From that moment on, Ravi had been sane and lucid again; a little balder for wear, but that was a small price to pay for the purity of his soul.

Sheila had been on a nearby hillock at the time. I know this because I could see her from the adjacent rice field. She had been contorting herself, pensively, in the old India-man ways, like a yogic maharishi reborn in a young girl's body. While her half brother was being possessed and tormented by the Dutchman, she was busy offering sun salutations to a crescent moon.

That was the year Sheila had been sent away to boarding school in Georgetown, and two years before I left Guyana.

I didn't see her again until we met years later at a *puja* in New York. It was odd that she was there, since she was more Portuguese Brazilian, from her father's side, than Indian. But I guess a little taste of the yogic trance had brought her back for more.

I took her to brunch the next day: scrambled eggs, toast and marmalade at Bregman's Eatery on 14th Street. That combination always took me back to Guyana, to the days of Empire and British propriety. With every mouthful of cholesterol poisoning came a gastronomically induced vision of Paddington station, chimeric regality, turban-clad soldiers and uncounted alien lands upon whose shores a thin layer of post-Cromwellian administration had been painted.

And were we not exemplary of such a thing, Sheila and I? The displaced Indian, perversely living vicariously through the blood of a pen, and through the lasting propaganda of a long-dead Empire; and the forgotten woman of mixed parentage and ghostly experiences: we were children of the melange.

We spoke of Back Home, of the crumbling sea wall that once was blinding in its white newness; of the sweet salt water, once clear like an albino baby's irises, now caked and clouded; and of the torrents of misshapen faces that had washed over us in youth. Old Millie, Sheila's mother, had moved to Toronto with the balding Ravi. Lal Bharat had wandered away, perhaps back to Surinam. And Long Baba had gone to join the spirit of the Dutchman.

Sheila's face was long and taut, chiselled like a man's. Her hair, like so many handfuls of black licorice, hung sourly by her pocked and brittle cheeks. She spoke sparingly, bu when she did, it was with deliberate purpose and intensity, as if her tongue had time only for the most important of vocalizations.

"I like to clean public washrooms," she said.

Another man, perhaps, would have been somewhat unnerved, maybe even amused. I just nodded, accepting it as yet another improper piece in a defective jigsaw puzzle.

"There's no better way to learn about a place," she continued, "than to snoop about its public toilets. The graffiti, the brand of soap. The stains."

I nodded, not caring to hear any more. All the girls back on 4th Street, from which both Sheila and I had come, talked like that: full of sarcasm and erratic humour. But Sheila was a grown woman now, with much time spent in America. The certainty of her sarcasm left me.

"I met my last boyfriend while cleaning the men's room at Wen Chung's," she said. "He wasn't at all surprised to see me."

"What did you say to him?" I asked.

"I told him I'd been searching all my life for the man who could piss straight and blow his nose at the same time."

And?

"And so he did," she said. Love at first sight, I thought.

She was so much like Ravi, Sheila was, so much the vulgar princess, intruder into the unknown. She, too, would have uncorked that bottle, knowing full well the potential dangers. I watched her bite into a succulent mango without cutting it or removing the skin: another demonstration of her attraction to the uncouth.

"The sour must be juxtaposed atop the sweet," she gurgled. Green juice crawled down her jaw like the aftermath to a wild animal's feast. I was reminded of an Argentinean science-fiction film in which orgasmic alien women exuded blue fluids from their mouths. I remembered, too, Sheila's jagged contortions atop the hillock overlooking Ravi's possession scene: so much like an alien sex ritual, yet ironically more a part of my culture than of her own.

She wiped the green from her mouth, and took my arm. We left Bregman's and walked to the harbour, drawn by an ancestral memory, a primal instinct. Ports and port towns have always beckoned we Guyanese, as if that fishy salty air were a kind of spiritual nutrition.

I had been walking along the river that other night, too, shortly before Ravi's ghostly encounter, on my way to the rice field by the hillock. On my walk, I had seen old Bhaji teetering and mumbling as usual, his breath's ethanol scent mixing poorly with the river's more pungent odours.

He had thrown something small into the raging water, something fragile and sickly. He had then saluted the sinking package and burst into a drunken rendition of "God Save the Queen."

It was an emaciated dog, I realized, as the package squirmed briefly. Bhaji had been paid in rum to do what the dog's owners were too cowardly to do themselves.

He had looked at me then, pausing in his awful song, and had called out to me clearly across the cooling wet air: "The sun always sets when there is fear of tigers!" It was an old Indian proverb, of course, connoting that bad things happen at once.

Soon followed the episode by the sea wall, and the eerie vision of stickly Sheila bent and twisted in the cleansing positions. Her poses had mirrored Ravi's racked posture, as if both siblings suffered the spectral possession together, linked by that psychic sub-ether that is never fully doubted in the lands of coconut trees and warm salt water.

I had been entranced by the sight of her, though I could not know of the drama played out beyond the hillock. Her sexless mannish body had bent backwards ninety degrees at the pelvis, a claymation puppet dangled from the stars, defying the very Newtonian force that imprisoned her alien form here within our gravity well.

I could almost feel the supreme ecstasy of her stretch: the separation of muscle fibres between her shoulder blades, the lengthening of connective tissues along her spine, and the distancing of vertebrae in her lower back. I was empathically drawn to her expressive relaxation, a release of pure chemical pleasure that brought me sexual attraction to a very unfeminine form.

And I had shuddered.

"I never had sex in a public washroom, if that's what you're thinking," Sheila said to me. I shuddered again, this time more against the cold of the Manhattan harbour. I wished she would stop.

She said nothing more. We stood there for some minutes, huddled against the icy breeze, leaning against the railing, and pushing our noses toward the Atlantic. Beneath us, bits of refuse floated by, buoyed by the density of sludge and sewage that masqueraded as Caribbean mud.

Sheila produced a bottle from inside her coat, then reached over and plucked a hair from the crown of my head. I winced and recoiled, my patience for her insanity dwindling by the minute. She placed the hair, with one of her own, inside the bottle, corked it, then tossed it into the water.

"After Long Baba threw the Dutchman's bottle over the sea wall," I said, "you fished it out and opened it. Right?" She nodded, but she could have been lying. It's a reasonable thing to do, I suppose, to blame one's derangement on demonic possession.

We stood there for a while, silent, and I watched her. She was lost in memory, perhaps recollecting that night atop the hillock, or countless bathroom encounters. Me, I was warmed by the digesting marmalade in my belly, and by the knowledge that I was far from a place where tigers are feared after sunset.

From the corner of Sheila's mouth, like a slash across her jugular or the slithering shade of a phantasmic influence, a line of green mango juice crawled down her throat.

Nataraj

THROUGH TIGHTENED eyelids, he could sense a sea of stars beyond the thatched roof of the hut. The astrological dance progressed smoothly, Venus rising in the constellation Leo, while planets moved west to east, then doubled back upon their paths. Pinned to a swinging pendulum, a mass of humanity lay flat against the Earth, spinning unnoticeably.

Thanaj lay on a bed of hay, his eyes tightly shut. In the morning there would be a haze as the mists rose from the bog, and there would be noise when the animals brayed and the villagers woke for another day of work. Until then there would be silence and the odour of night. He felt the motion of the Earth, its race through space while tethered to the sun. In a few hours, he would march to the rice fields to toil ankle-deep in water, then slink back to be with Shakira, enjoy her meal. He would then slip gratefully back into the circuitous swim through dream space.

He would feel the spin of the Earth three more times before Shakira gave birth.

Thanaj was not present when his son was born, for the rice fields had beckoned, and the harvest would not wait for fatherhood. But he had left word for the child to be named Nataraj for that aspect of divine Shiva who danced the universe anew with every celestial epoch. There had been no fear that it would be a girl child, for Shakira had carried it low, and guru-ji's metal pendulum would rotate counter-clockwise when held above the swelling belly: clear indications of the coming of a son.

When the day's harvest was done, Thanaj rushed back through the darkness to hold his wife and child, and to hear every word of the tale of Nataraj's birth: As the sun had climbed to its apex high in the sky, Shakira had wailed in the agony of childbirth, as her mother and grandmothers had done before her. She had panted and pushed, had felt the ripping of baby's flesh from her own. She had held Nataraj against her heaving bosom as she awaited the afterbirth, had wiped the wetness from his eyes and had bathed in the glory of his wails.

Thanaj beamed anew as his child cried again. This was the ritual of arrival, he was convinced, the announcement of great potential. In whatever language they spoke, or through whatever reasoning they brought with them from the previous life, it was all babies' privilege to scream their identities with their first lungfull of terrestrial air. It was with the passing days and weeks that memories of previous lives, knowledge of the karmic debts to be paid and collected, faded behind the veil of material life.

As those days and weeks passed, Nataraj grew quickly. In the first year, he took ill only once, though six other village children born that year perished from various maladies. He would not remember that year, nor the next three, ever again. But their influence would be felt through all aspects of Nataraj's material existence.

Mother is a child's word for God, and Nataraj slowly separated himself from his God, making way for Shakira to give birth to four more children, two of which would die before Nataraj saw his sixth year. He was left with two younger sisters: Sushita and Mala.

As his body grew and his awareness matured, he saw himself in truthful light: a small lithe boy with bad skin and an unremarkable face. It wasn't until his eighth year that the darkness of his skin was apparent, darker than that of the families who lived higher on the village slope. The children he saw in the schoolhouse were dark like him, but there were others who were not. Those others he would see when walking to school; they were dressed in fine whites and scarves, and would diverge from the schoolhouse road to travel elsewhere with their bags and books.

The whisperings were many, but there were no facts forthcoming. Most intriguing of all were the fair girls who would grip their grey skirts with one hand and their brothers' arms with the other. Cleaner, better and more mysterious, they drew his eye more than did the simpler girls of his own kind.

Inspired by the passings of these clean, crisp and feminine forms, the stirrings in his loins doubled in intensity daily, and relief could only be found by his own hand. The fruitless spillage of semen is a ritual that young men cannot escape, one that reminds them of the limitations and foibles of the physical body, and an indicator of gross metabolic changes that harken to the onslaught of adulthood.

In time, Thanaj brought Nataraj to the fields with him on alternate days, and Nataraj learned the joy and agony that was his father's existence. There would come a day, he was reminded regularly, when he would be pulled from the regimented dry and cool schoolhouse to toil daily in the fields, and those exciting, terrifying and lengthy days of childish delight would remain as but a memory. Until then he was to learn as much as he could, driven by a fear of indolence and a desire to better himself.

Of greatest importance in those years were the days of adventure with the other village boys. In those instances, Nataraj would learn how to hunt insects, how to fight and excel physically. He would also learn, from stories told from stories, of the secrets of female anatomy, and of the glories of the great world that stretched beyond the valley.

In was an unremarkable day when Parvin was brought to him with her parents. He was pulled from his homework and introduced to the family. He had seen her about, but had never before spoken to her. She was two years younger, and somewhat plain, but not objectionable. They were told to clasp hands while the fathers conducted the appropriate rites. He looked to her eyes, and she lowered hers. Within the hour, the visiting family was gone, and Nataraj returned to his books. But he was now betrothed.

With beckoning adulthood, Nataraj was taken by his father to the temples with greater rigour. There, the brahmins would recite for him the *vedas*, and Thanaj would slap his son's knee whenever some words of particular import were spoken. *Puja* was performed for him regularly now, and Thanaj was desperate to convince his son of the importance of spiritual purity.

"We are all born with the burdens of our past lives," Thanaj would tell him. "By performing our duties we can assure rebirth into lives of wealth and pleasure."

"And to be freed from rebirth?" Nataraj asked once.

"Would take many lives of effort. Best you spend this life making up for the last."

Some nights, he would lie with Thanaj atop piles of cloth and stare up into the night sky. Father and son felt the spin of the Earth together and suffered celestial torments and astrological decrees. It was the stars that had declared Parvin to be an acceptable match; it was the sun and moon that compelled the seasons and the harvest.

Muscle rested comfortably atop Nataraj's shoulders and back, and hair darkened his face, chest and pubis. A willowy summer month saw two important moments in his life: his removal from school to work the fields full-time, and his marriage to Parvin. With the latter event came the penultimate separation from Mother-God, and Shakira had wept alone on her son's wedding night.

It would be for Nataraj to weep the following month, though. Under that same sun that had nurtured, warmed, fed, withered and melted his grandfathers, Thanaj dropped to his knees in the rice fields, swooned, and slipped from mortality within the hour.

". . . Returned to the cycle," Nataraj had said as he watched his father's body burn in the cremation fire. True to his name, he had focused his mind on the image of dancing Shiva, with the drum of creation in one hand and the torch of destruction in the other. Still, the anguish choked him, for never again would he lay with his father beneath the stars. Nataraj was now husband to his own wife, protector to his mother, and father to his sisters. The ecstatic wisdom of Thanaj was lost to him forever.

In a home with four women, Nataraj was driven to solitude, choosing to lie alone at night outside the hut. To watch the sky turn for an hour before drifting into dream space was his one connection to Thanaj, the father who had left no photos, no mementos, only a void and an echoing voice.

As his need demanded, he would lie with Parvin, and soon her belly swelled high with a female child. But unlike his father, Nataraj was able to be present at the birth of his daughter whom he named Shanti. He gripped her tiny form to his chest, and she roared with bestial rage about indignities that only newborns understand. In a few weeks, she would forget the secret knowledge she now possessed, thrust back to this world of sensation for yet another lifetime. Nataraj cooed this into her wet ear, trying to convince his daughter that he, too, was privy to that secret knowledge.

He would not stare at the night sky with Shanti, nor with any of his subsequent seven children. Instead, he would reserve that experience for himself alone. For during the day he was compelled to look at the ground, to the rice paddies and to the feet of the other villagers working there. His walk home each night, and the time spent staring up from his bed, were his moments of solitary contemplation.

In time, he arranged for the marriages of his sisters, and his home was now the sole domain of Parvin, Shakira and his many offspring. It was a place of little peace in those days of small children, and he took to languishing on the paths longer than was necessary. There, he would often catch glimpses of the fairer people in their finery, going, he assumed, to and from the city.

As they had in their youth, they shone with clear skin, unmarked clothes and confidence. The same sun that had desiccated old Thanaj's scalp and shoulders had softened their faces and lightened their hair. As he had so many years ago, Nataraj stopped to breathe in the brilliance of the fair women. His own body was now hard and black, his hair matted and unkempt. Gone were the cinematic eyes that had once beamed from his childish head, replaced now with the wise and weathered brow of a rice farmer. But behind those eyes still revelled the spirit that had erupted from Shakira's womb decades ago, still seeking fulfilment, knowledge, and even adventure.

He was thankful for Parvin, for her strength, wisdom and dependability. But he was drawn away to another world when he contemplated those other women. It was, after all, beyond him to leave the village and his family. He was bound here by commitments, tradition and . . . fear. Yet, like the great insect hunts of his youth, an adventurous spirit demanded action.

Each day for a month he would stop at that same spot by the path and watch a certain skirted woman walk down the hill from the bus stop to the upper fringes of their village. Her name he must have heard before, even as they were children, but he could not remember it. He could not arrive to see her leave in the mornings, for he was already in the fields by then. But he would always be there to witness her arrival in early evening.

He began to pretend that she was coming home to him, to tell him of her exciting day in the city. He devised complex conversations she would have with him, fantasized about their illusory family and his elevated status. At no time did she look at him, acknowledge his presence or slow in her rush to get home. When it became clear that she would never pause even to look into his eyes, Nataraj was remorseful. He concluded that there is nothing worse in the universe than unfulfilled desire, hopelessness.

When his youngest child, Gita, died of a common malady, Nataraj put his fantasies aside, and was abashed at ever having had them. He discovered, in the most painful way, that there is indeed something worse than unfulfilled desire.

That same year Mother Shakira breathed her last. She had always been joyful and remained thankful until the end for a long life filled with a fine husband, children and many grandchildren. The evening she died, the stars had stood still, and the world ceased to turn but for a moment. In that moment, Shiva did not dance, and a hole was carved out from Nataraj's heart.

To be forsaken by a lover is heartbreaking, and by a father is tragic. When Mother is lost, so is a child's God, and Nataraj felt that his soul was alone and cold. From the moment of his life's inception, his flesh had been tied to hers, though he had been taught that his spirit had come from elsewhere. "Today," he said aloud, "today I begin to die."

Many years ago, Thanaj had told his son about how he had felt when his own parents had died. "Who will look after me now?" Thanaj had said. "But I was already twenty-four years old." The same sense had settled upon Nataraj, who felt the beast of ultimate responsibility shifting restlessly upon his shoulders.

"I will look after you now," Parvin said, as if in answer. She took him beneath her wing along with her children, and expanded to fill the space left by Mother Shakira.

When Shanti was married and brought her children to see their grandparents, Nataraj's jaw swelled with pride, and he sometimes caught himself unconsciously emulating Thanaj's postures and sounds. A little belly had long been dipping over the edge of his tightly tied *lungi*, but recently he had given up trying to suck it back. Now he revelled in the status granted him by the grey in his hair, the toothlessness of his grin, and the awkwardness of his swagger.

To his last day, Thanaj had bent in the rice fields. The pain in his back and in his swollen knees allowed Nataraj to avoid that fate. He retired to the same hut in which he had been born, in which he had raised eight children, and where the families of his two sons now resided. There he would watch the sun rise and set each day, and he would track the phases of the moon each month.

On a cloudless night, he beckoned Parvin to join him on a pile of cloth outside. There, arm in arm, they watched the constellations glide through the heavens, until they both slipped into blissful sleep. Once more, Nataraj travelled the dreamscape, running painlessly on odourless meadows and hunting insects with childhood friends. In that brightly coloured universe, he lay with Thanaj again and was drawn to Mother Shakira's bosom endlessly, lured to a realm devoid of physical meaning or material consequence.

During the voyage, his material body finally failed and his heart stopped beating.

He walked past the fair girl in the grey skirt while on his way to school. She looked into his eyes and smiled. He smiled back but kept on walking, hand-in-hand with Parvin. They ran along together behind Thanaj who made them chase the setting sun over a green hillock where, waiting with a grand picnic, was smiling and joyful Shakira.

He was drawn about them, through them and around them. The sun faded to a bed of lights, stars, and he counted constellations until the lids of his eyes could restrain his fatigue no longer. In the dream of dreams, he fell asleep.

When he opened his eyes again, he was in the arms of a midwife, and was being handed to a new mother, doted over by a new father. And he cried loudly and profoundly for having been returned yet again to this material world, away from a perfect embrace.

King Rice

OKAY, THIS is what we Creole-speakers call a long-time story, something that happened a good many years ago. It's about a man named Bungy, or at least that's what people call him. Back Home, nobody really knows anybody's real name, and if they do, they never admit to it in polite company. So, as far as anyone need know, this man's name was Bungy.

I should know a little something about Bungy, since he is, after all, almost family. My mother's brother married a woman whose cousin's granddaddy was, you know, Bungy. So he is almost family.

Now, Bungy was one funny man. That's the way my daddy describes him. To men of my daddy's generation, anybody willing to make a fool of himself is a funny man ranked high with the likes of Milton Berle and Jack Benny. It occurs to me now that maybe Bungy was a little sick in the head, like North American big-city people who holler at phantoms and direct imaginary traffic.

In Guyana, though, no one's mad if he can feed himself. It's a good rule to control the number of loons in the bin.

Maybe Bungy wasn't so much mad as he was daunting, the way bank robbers and Evil Knievel are. A psychiatrist friend told me once that that kind of people are called "psychopaths," a term usually associated with criminals, though most of them never get around to actually committing a crime. So maybe Bungy was a psychopath, but one fully able to feed himself.

Now, the entire village was mad for cricket. The Windsor Forest team, despite being made up of underfed farmers and farmers' sons, had been making dramatic gains on the national circuit. Every man and every man's son came out to cheer them on, for they represented, not only the proud dung-ridden west-coast village of Windsor Forest, but all villagers who owned and worked their own land.

Bungy, of course, was madder for cricket than most.

Bungy went to every single game, regardless of the distance he had to travel. That was also the magic of the day; cricket gods unfailingly allowed for good weather during game days, so that the most psychopathic of fans could cycle through the mud-gutted unpaved roads to cheer on their feckless heroes. Bungy would push that old bicycle to its rusted physical limits, packing a lunch and a cricket bat (which, of course, required him to steer dangerously with one hand for the entire journey) so that nothing, not hunger nor an obstructing head, could deny him the pleasure of witnessing firsthand a Windsor Forest victory.

Bungy was so fanatical, in fact, that he had been known to be provoked to physical violence if his team were slandered in even the mildest of ways. And this was many decades before British football hooliganism, let me tell you. This was something *we* gave to the English.

My mother's brother, who would later marry Bungy's grandson's cousin, told me that Bungy at one time threw him from Bungy's house because he had *implied* that maybe, perchance, by the will of God, it was conceivable the Windsor Forest team might fail to win the Demerara Cup that year. Not even deference to the will of God had been sufficient to quell the ire of our man Bungy.

So the *grande finale* approached: the final match between the rice farmers of Windsor Forest and the sugar plantation workers of neighbouring Eyeflood. It was a poetic ending to a versified season indeed, as this match-up would pit the imperialist-sponsored sugar team against our intrepid heroes from the autonomous mudlands.

And the venue would be the enemy's home fortress, the Eyeflood Cricket Grounds, built and maintained splendidly with imperialist sugar money; a far cry from the dung-scattered sandtrap against the seawall back in Windsor Forest. Back Home, the practices had to be cut short twice a day because the rising water level made it a submarine game. Not many people have played cricket well *under* the Caribbean.

No, the odds were definitely against the rice farmers this time. But there was confidence all around, because the rallying power of Bungy's madness was renowned and highly revered by supporters and antagonists alike. The team itself was wary of playing if any rumour reached them that, for whatever reason, Bungy would not be in the stands inciting lunacy.

Perhaps I've not stressed sufficiently the uniqueness of Bungy's dementia, the humour of his approach. Back when Mr Carruthers, the brand-new Governor General of Her Majesty's Guyanese Territories, had first risen to power, he decided to celebrate his recent appointment by personally visiting every last miserable village under the Queen's protection. The villagers had dressed in their Sunday best and politely lined up to shake the undoubtedly distinguished hand of Lord Carruthers.

Bungy had not disappointed. He, too, had dusted off his suit, lain unused since he had had to appear in court many years ago on an unsubstantiated public indecency charge. Instead of a tie, though, he had worn about his neck, for the plain view of Lord Carruthers, a noose fashioned from the finest Indian jute.

"Why are you wearing a noose about your neck?" Carruthers had foolishly inquired.

"Because I, Sir," Bungy had replied, full of airs, "am a slave."

On another occasion, Bungy found himself in the capital city, Georgetown, with no money to get home again. Luckily, he was aware that my mother's brother's future wife's cousin was visiting in the nearby town of Lenora, equipped with a very useful automobile.

So Bungy, penniless, boarded the bus bound for Lenora and waited for his stop. When it was time to pay, he ambushed the ticket collector, crying, "Is this *Ninora*? I have to be in *Ninora* to be in court!"

"You fool," the collector had said, "you're in *Lenora*!"

"Oh no!" Bungy had exclaimed. "You'd better let me out!" The driver complied, and so Bungy had managed to get himself a free ride to his grandson's auto.

With such precedents, it wasn't surprising that the gathered onlookers expected much from our hero. Not just that he would serve to entertain them during the duller moments of an otherwise gripping cricket match, but that, in the event of athletic tragedy, Bungy would be able to lift his team's spirits from the clean-swept Eyeflood field and onwards unto victory.

And so, on the grand day in question, the Windsor Forest contingent had been nervously silent until the appearance of the fabled Bungy, who had arrived uncharacteristically late. He had walked there, leaving his bicycle at home, and was curiously without his lucky cricket bat. This was enough to set some players and spectators aback, to be sure, but they were quelled by the sight of Bungy's little brown bag. At least he had brought his lunch, they saw, so some holy customs were to be maintained.

The game went off to a terrible start. The Eyeflood team, their brilliant white cotton uniforms blinding in the tropical sun, terrorized the awestricken lads from

Windsor Forest. Our champion bowler, Big Castro, actually missed the wicket on two occasions. And the rice fields' favourite son, James Caan Number Two, bungled at least three easy catches. The sun was in his eye, onlookers said, no doubt reflected off those overstarched Eyeflood shirts.

The boys were bumbling and fumbling, their muscles tight with fright. As one miserable beast, their pleading eyes looked up to the stands, meeting those of solemn-faced Bungy. His forehead was creased in vexation, his lips pursed in sobriety.

Then, without warning, he stood and raised his paper bag before him. The crowd went silent, and even the players paused anxiously in their match. From somewhere off in the adjacent meadow, a cow was heard to bray, a curiously melodic note against the rhythmic background of Caribbean waves.

Bungy reached into his bag and pulled out a handful of the finest Guyanese rice he could have purchased, grown, no doubt, in the muddy fields of Windsor Forest. He scattered them over his audience, bellowing: "King rice!" Then, in a more guttural tone, he gestured to the bewildered Eyeflood team and cursed: "Slave sugar."

A resounding cheer erupted from the stands, drowning the feeble protestations of the very proper Eyeflood backers. Big Castro screwed up his courage and bowled straight from then on, and James Caan Number Two made the most thrilling catch anyone had ever seen.

The Demerara Cup still went to Eyeflood that year. But nobody ever forgot the brilliant madness of Bungy, my mother's brother's wife's cousin's granddaddy.

Far from Family

SOMETIMES FEROZE would clutch the sides of his head and think about twisting off his own neck, like he saw once in a strikingly vivid Hong Kong martial arts film. It wasn't a prepubescent deathwish, or an expression of Hemingway-style machismo unlikely for a ten-year-old, but simply an act of boredom.

He was convinced that regular daily neck twists, vigorous of course would eventually allow him to look backwards, 180 degrees, like an owl.

"The boy will break he neck!" Uncle Mustafah would exclaim to his wife. "Look at that damn-silly boy. He go twist off he own head, then he mumma will take *me* to task!"

At such times, Auntie Farah would suck her teeth and sputter at Mustafah without even looking up. "Quiet, na! The boy's not able to break his own bloody neck. Not unless you help him. Then his mumma will tar your backside for sure."

This particular summer afternoon, however, Feroze quickly became bored of self-decapitation and decided that he would teach himself to fly. He dashed down the thin hall of Uncle and Auntie's suburban bungalow, leaping at every fifth step. With each leap, he soared higher. It was only a matter of time and practice, he told himself, before he would be able to sail across the sky alongside the birds.

"Well, na, look at that boy!" Uncle Mustafah dropped his newspaper. "Ten damn-silly years old, and he think he able to fly. That boy's not good in he head!"

"Then maybe you shoulda let him twist it off," Auntie Farah said. Not once during the exchange did she look up from her magazine. In her keen mind's eye, the events within her own household were played out with Stratfordian vividness; she had no need of actually seeing her husband and nephew.

"Feroze!" Uncle Mustafah barked. "What if you hit you head, eh? What will you mumma say to me then?"

"Okay, Uncle," Feroze said. "I'll go downstairs."

"Hmmph," Uncle Mustafah said, disarmed by the boy's unexpected obedience. "Just don't try flyin' in the basement," he said more softly. "Damn-silly boy."

Feroze was more than willing to abandon his aerodynamic experiments for the moment. The austere basement, usually a forbidden place in which to play, promised greater stimulation.

There were no basements back in Trinidad, Daddy had said once. Back home, he had said, the sea would rise too often during the year, and anybody damn-silly enough to dig a basement would see his whole house float away! He said that most of the houses were propped up on stilts, which had seemed to Feroze to be a very entertaining prospect.

His cheeks brightened at the prospect of frolicsome play. Imagine the kind of diving and fishing one could do from one's own front door! The image tickled him for days, until he had overheard his parents recollecting a long-time story of when Millie, an elderly neighbour, had been washed away to sea during one of the floods.

Since then, the reveries about stilted houses had remained quietly in repose, hidden somewhere in the archives of his brain. He was reluctant to let those houses go completely, regardless of their odious connection to drowned old ladies. They were one of the last images given to him by his daddy before a slippery road and faulty brakes had left him and his mumma alone.

The resilience of youth shielded him then, as he descended the bungalow stairs. Death, anger, sickness, and loneliness are all quick darts whose pain is to be endured an instant, but whose effects are felt long afterwards; there were more immediate matters to consider. Such is the strength of childhood, that all mortal distractions could themselves be diverted by simply inventing adventure. And so an epic Arthurian quest was begun, as heroic young Feroze crawled expectantly towards Uncle Mustafah's secret dust-ridden chest.

The thing had lain there for as long as Feroze could remember. He knew that Uncle and Auntie had brought it from Trinidad, and that Granddaddy had brought it there from India before. Feroze had never been allowed to see what was inside, and had never asked. Though sometimes at night, when he was supposed to be asleep, he had heard Mumma and Uncle and Auntie rummaging through it, laughing and sometimes crying.

In the chest lay power. A strange kind of power, not like Merlin's wand or Rama's bow or Suleyman's word. The chest was evil, he was sure, because it preferred to lie in the dusty shadows of Uncle's basement, where the odours of incense had settled and the colours of worthless Caribbean paintings had faded and caked upon the floor.

Instruments of white magic would certainly glisten in the darkness like the crescent moon against the black cloak of night. They would give a ping when touched, flourish when wielded, and blazon with thunder and fire when invoked.

He was fascinated by the chest and by its influence. This old black leather box, from a dirty and forgotten country, exuded subtle and evil magic which had aroused his family's sentiments. Anything that indirect, he reasoned, was hopelessly cowardly. And anything embodying such cowardice, Daddy had once implied, was no good to anybody.

Venomously, the chest hissed through its imagined reptilian aura and poisoned air. In the lightless nether region of the basement, Feroze fought the tidal wave of terror that constricted his throat and taunted him in a way that only imaginative children understand; he was compelled to continue, but the very thing that made his quest bewitching terrorized his ten-year-old heart.

But he pushed mindless terror from his thoughts, as Daddy had once insisted when the power had gone out one night. "The *jumbies* are like bad dogs," he had said. "They can smell it when you're afraid. So *act* brave, and you will *be* brave."

He flung the lid of the chest open. Inside were not the decaying bones of prehistoric dragons, nor the silken capes of some undead sorcerer; only photographs, littered about inside the chest like autumn leaves on the front lawn.

Some were recent, from the last ten years. Feroze could tell, because he recognized himself in these few, his gawking brown child's eyes beaming back at the camera like a ghost from his past, peering back at him through the lens in a twisted, knowing grin.

The rest were ancient and precious, all originally black and white, some coloured by hand like photos in the old *National Geographics* in Uncle and Auntie's dining room. Many were of his dead daddy, a face almost forgotten now that years had filled the emptiness he had left behind. Feroze lingered upon these awhile, but found no comfort in them. The man they portrayed sometimes semiclothed, often adrift upon a fishing raft, or drinking rum on the porch of a stilted house, was a stranger to him and brought him no closer to the lost philosophy that was his father.

But many of the other photos, most of these torn and taped back together as if someone had pretended to discard them, were of a man Feroze had never seen before. The Indian man was tall and skinny, good looking the way scrawny rock 'n' roll stars were supposed to be good looking. His black hair was oiled in every picture and pleated flat against his scalp. One photo that caught Feroze's eye was of this man, bedecked only in a *lungi* and a scheming smile, adorning a Trinidadian beach with a pretty mulatto girl on each arm.

In every picture, the stranger beamed, brighter than the tropical sun that fed his warmth. His features were similar to those of Feroze's father in youth, though darker and leaner. And behind those smiling eyes floated a distracted brooding entity, poised precariously between play and design.

On the back of the beach photo was an inscription: *Raj and his friends, April 16, 1968*

Feroze could not have recognized the handwriting, that of a poorly educated Caribbean Creole-speaker, taking great pains to demonstrate penmanship skills inherited from the British system. But he had once heard someone allude to such a thing: an echoing voice cursing ``impositions'' and ``imperialists incursions''; possibly the voice of his daddy or one of his countless forgotten uncles.

He did recognize the gummy India Ink, typical of all his parents' documents; and the big flourishing R's, his mother's trademark.

But who was Raj? Most Indian men from Trinidad looked pretty much the same, since they were all supposedly descended from common stock. That's what Daddy had said: they all came over on the same few ships from India back when the English were looking for cheap labour.

``Feroze?'' came a hesitant call from upstairs. ``What you doing?''

"Nothing, Uncle!" Feroze called back, slamming shut the lid of the chest. He had neglected to put away the photo of Raj, so it lay conspicuously by his knee as Mustafah cautiously made his way downstairs.

Surprisingly, Uncle was not angry. But on his face were etched the lines of grandfatherly concern that usually caused adventure and jollity to flee from Feroze's heart. "You see him, na? You Uncle Raj." Mustafah sat cross-legged on the floor next to Feroze.

"Uncle," Feroze said. "Who is Raj?"

"You daddy's brother, boy. Bad news, that Raj, bad news." Uncle Mustafah creased his lips and nodded solemnly, contemplating past pain.

"How come?"

"Break you daddy's heart, na. If he mumma been alive, he woulda break she heart, too."

Feroze gazed at Raj's visage, entranced by its genial facade. The distant eyes sprang forth from the photo, traversing oceans of water and time, to seize his nephew's imagination. Had this beaming man been evil? But evil men don't smile so openly; everybody knew that.

What had he done?

"Fightin' and wildin' in the street, that boy," Mustafah said. "Just like you daddy." He laughed, the lines in his forehead smoothing over, his waxen face flushed with the aura of memory.

"Did Raj kill somebody?" Feroze asked.

"Na. He na kill nobody." Mustafah thought for a second, the magical aura gone now, replaced with a hue of vexation and analytical recall. "Far as m' know, he na kill nobody."

There was never a time when Feroze had not known Mustafah to be a shabby old man, full of anger at the young, of yearning for the old, and of resentment of the middle-aged and successful. Especially when his words were of death and killing, the ripples beneath his eyes seemed to deepen, and his eyeballs receded further into his skull, as if he aged another twenty years each time he pondered a death.

Mustafah was silent now, almost oblivious to Feroze's presence. He was far away. This was more sadness to settle like dirty snow upon his family's house, to push down on the foundations, chilling their bones and drying their air.

What had Raj done?

"He na do nothin', boy," Mustafah said suddenly, his hard skin cracked with a forced smile. "Nothin' that you got fo' know about." He rose quickly and hobbled up the stairs as briskly as he could. The old stairs creaked as if they were going to break. But they always made that noise and yet were as strong as the day they were first built.

Feroze immediately dove back into the chest. Perhaps within its guarded interior he could find a clue to Raj's mysterious life.

Pushing through its priceless booty was like cowboy archaeology. Feroze was Indiana Jones of the old photographs. Two hands were folded in inverted prayer, forced down through the pile, then pushed outward to sift through the disturbed reservoir of Kodak paper.

An edge brushed by his left thumb, pressing hard against his soft brown flesh, sawing across the microscopic valleys and mountains that formed his fingerprints. A line of blood slipped along the fissure, mingling with the silver nitrates in the chest, enhancing the treasure a thousandfold.

His eyebrows creased in pain, then relaxed as the sharpness relented. The mixing continued, and drops of his blood beaded upon several glossy surfaces like tears on the freshly waxed kitchen floor. His fingers seized upon a new surface, rough and old, yellow and fragile. He gingerly lifted it from the assortment, careful not to let his trickling blood be spread upon it.

It was a birth certificate, handwritten and quite ancient. Raj Kumar Bengir, born June 13, 1951, Port of Spain, Trinidad & Tobago. Mother: Alya Bengir, housewife. Father: Lal Bengir, general labourer.

He put the birth certificate aside and placed his cut finger inside his mouth.

Salt! Like the dry desert sands of northwestern India, like the brine waters that washed the beaches of Trinidad. The taste of blood was strange to his tongue, though familiar to an elusive part of him.

He forged on through Solomon's mines, the sacred stockpile of family recollection. In it, he found four faded Caribbean passports; tickets of release, further magic items that had transported his family across oceans and continents.

But that was all. There was no more.

Raj was a criminal, it was clear. A thief and a murderer, like all those loud swaggering Trinidadian men.

Through squinted eyes, the scene is blurred, and Feroze flies amongst the birds. He soars upon the wings of a child's paper airplane, borne over vast stretches of water and half a continent: a voyage much shortened by the space warp of imagination. Beneath him, an abscess on a calm blue face, rests a quizzical pointed island upon which a swarming body of ants sways with undulations.

Feroze sees the one ant who is unlike the others. It is alone and devious, locked into a circuitous hunt.

A black Indian panther on his turf, Raj stalks the pristine beaches, consuming rum and women like sickly and slow Asian deer. Muscled and directed, a machine of single intent, his body is bathed in its own salted sweat and the sweet liberated blood of others.

A blight upon the throbbing island, his predatory machinations are a deafening light in whose shadows the panther hunts with nose and eye. Feroze smells his musk, his salty breath, and tastes the playful hunger within him.

And what has happened to him?

Like all natural criminals, he is smuggled away to a far place. Maybe England. Maybe India.

The panther stalks anew in a richer land.

Feroze placed the things back into the chest. Driven to silence, he swooned as the stillness of the solitary basement submerged him. One last item was held back, though, cached in his pants' pocket, perhaps unconsciously.

He pushed the chest to its original resting spot, careful to leave everything the way he had found it. There was no Holy Grail here, no Solomon's Mines. Still, he would leave no trace of his passing.

He went back upstairs to find Uncle and Auntie slouching about, reading magazines. He sneaked up behind Mustafah and flung his arms about the old man's shoulders.

He smells the talc upon the wrinkled neck.

"Uncle," he whispers into Mustafah's ears. "Where is Raj?"

"He deh in England, boy." And Feroze smiles contentedly, knowing he has interpreted his vision correctly.

The gears of time still creak backwards in old Mustafah's head, though, conscious of tragedies and lies, responsibilities and the ties of blood. He is hardened by the deaths of family members: brothers by marriage and race. One is lost in a car accident while his wife and son wait at home. The other, tormented by a shrinking beach and the brevity of youth, drinks Paraquat and has his innards melted away by the herbicide. Such is the fate of an unthinking desperate panther.

Feroze's eyes glisten with the absorption of a false revelation. His black cat roams England still, flailing terror across the countryside, scratching paths to caches of buried demonic treasure.

In Feroze's back pocket rests the true prize, the egg from the treasure chest's nest: his father's passport. Detailed within the creased and blurry black & white photo are the lines of fatherly concern that marked his face until his end. But in the narrow grooves that emanate from the sides of the eyes, like rays of sunlight, Feroze sees the twinkle of ambition that had possessed his father, and had drawn him and his brood to a new home far from the islands, far from family.

The Rhymer

SOME MEN chanted and prayed, others played simple tunes, and the rest merely held out their hands and looked forlorn. Bort provided a unique service: he was a maker of rhymes.

Not just any rhymes, mind you; not simple, mindless poems designed by children's minds and cretins; nor the filth-ridden limericks that were so popular amongst the baser creed (at least not unless requested by the client). No. Bort's brand of rhyme, he felt, was profound in its austerity, penetrating in its continence, and fervid in its ardour.

While the others twiddled on their wooden flutes and bowed mechanically when the odd coin fell into their cups, or moaned pitiful but indistinct words of benediction upon the hand from which the reluctant coin fell, Bort would stretch his lungs and expel from them quatrains and verse unique to each client. He walked through the unclean streets like a philosopher king among beggars, greater than the rest, for he was not devoid of pride.

He earned a stipend.

Habib the butcher had paid his retainer this day. "Rhyme for me such that my meat will be sweet, and my profits sweeter," he had decreed. And Bort had not disappointed. Placing his left hand delicately at his throat, looking into the turquoise sky, and feeling the light breeze ruffle his tattered pant leg, Bort cleared his hungering throat and spoke:

O ye of fine dwellings and of choice flesh,

Whose touch of wood smellings and wire mesh

Upon which dead creatures and other such things

Are carved into cutlets for men fat as kings,

Good fate in thine quest

To sate all the gluttons

Who dine in their best

on beef, pork and mutton.

The beggars' moans had seemed to deepen. But Habib was pleased, or had at least failed to indicate otherwise. The glistening silver coin had flashed in the glorious sunlight and rung as the butcher flicked it into Bort's soft hand.

And with that perfect disk of precious metal, Bort the rhymer was able to purchase his daily meal of hard bread and lentil soup.

It was during the animated imbibing of that thick soup that a most unusual circumstance befell the rhymer. For years, convinced that he was the monarch of the streets, the sole possessor of artistic talent amongst a languid rabble of passionless hopeless urchins and freaks, Bort was struck with a vision as improbable as a satisfying dissonant rhyme.

What he saw, as gobs of lentil dribbled from his ragged beard, and as tactile yellow sunlight flooded into the spirited din of the morning marketplace, was a figure as penniless and listless as himself, draped similarly and possessing that which Bort had thought reserved for himself alone: pride.

She was a woman, though the shapeless unwashed clothing made that distinction difficult. Of an age close to that of the rhymer old, but young; young, but old she kept her black hair pleated closely against her sun-beaten scalp. She hovered serenely amongst the other mendicants, as expressionless as any princess, her posture erect and irreverent. And what was that seen to flicker across her simple features? Bort frowned and searched, unbelieving. Yes, it was true. For a brief moment lasting but a single heartbeat, and then shrouded by the brilliance of the early day, the suppliant princess had allowed herself to smile!

And such a smile! Not a guilty reward for having defied fate yet another day, nor a communicative gesture meant to mollify or please another, but a disgustingly curt self-gratifying inward-aiming grin of such intensity and assuredness that it made Bort sick. For the first time in his considerable life, Bort was unable to finish his meal.

What made this creature so arrogant?

The rhymer huffed and muttered to no one:

There goes a blithe vision,

A sorry one to see;

For what be her mission,

If not to disgrace me?

An eavesdropping passerby flipped an object in his direction; it was nothing more than a shiny bauble, a counterfeit coin. But Bort pocketed it nonetheless, grousing, "What can one expect for unsolicited work?" and received a grumble of assent from the assembled wretches.

Bort staggered to his feet, allowing dripping lentils to crash to the dirt where they were immediately pounced upon by salivating urchins. With the wonder, confusion, anger and shame of one whose universe has just been suddenly and inexplicably reworked, he forced foot to fall after foot as he trundled towards the interloper.

"Madam," he exclaimed, "I've not seen you here before."

The princess turned towards him, her head swivelling with perfect grace and immobile hair. Flaunting delicate eyebrows perched confidently atop a neutral yet amused little face, she asserted with an even, low-pitched voice that caused wonder to stir in the little hearts of the wretched observers: "And you must be the rhymer."

Bort paused for the most fleeting of moments to ponder the forceful voice. "Indeed," he said, "I am he. I've not seen you here before."

"You must be a poor rhymer in certainty, for you have spoke three sentences to me, and none of it has rhymed thus far." Was there a giggle from the gallery of miscreants that had assembled to observe their exchange? Surely it was just a trick of the wind whistling through the shards of someone's broken bowl of lentil soup.

Bort drew himself up to his full height, barely managing to rise above the interloper's scalp. "I've not seen you here before," he said, not totally devoid of pique. "If you wish me to rhyme," he continued, "you shall have to purchase my services."

The princess smiled again. This time it was not the stolen interior simper Bort had witnessed earlier, but a premeditated and directed sneer of such pomposity that the tattered front row shielded their eyes and stumbled back a step.

"My name is Arjazet," she spoke. "I am a teller of tales, a weaver of verbal yarns and a chronicler of worthy events." She flowed in her rent fabrics, causing them to swell like an empress's train. "And I have the means to pay you." She produced a shiny glass marble, a common marketplace charm popular among merchants' wives whose husbands suffered from idle moderate wealth.

The onlookers gasped.

"Rhyme for me, Bort."

Bort eyed the fake jewel cautiously. He had no need for such things; his preference was for real currency, with which hard bread and lentil soup could be obtained. But this glass marble, this valueless adornment from the fatuous bazaar would serve as the Indian jewel in his beggar's crown: a symbol of the pointless impetuousness of abrasive arrogance from the likes of Arjazet.

"I shall rhyme for you, princess," he said. "But you must also tell me a tale."

"Done!" cried Arjazet. "However, I am no charitable company. I do not share of my produce freely. What have you to offer me in return for my service?"

Bort dug about in his pockets and discovered the bauble that had been tossed to him in the eatery. "I offer this shiny counterfeit coin," he said.

Arjazet inspected the offering from afar, smirked, then nodded assent. She had not said a word, but her meaning was fluent: "If that's all you can manage, then it will have to do."

"I don't usually rhyme for toys," Bort continued, "so this had better be worth my while."

At last! The abominable woman was rendered truly speechless! "I propose," Bort said, "that the response of our audience decide whose presentation is the better. The winner keeps both prizes, and the loser must abase *her*self before the victor this day and for all days to come."

"Fair enough!" Arjazet said. "The loser will abase *him*self before the victor. There can be but one philosopher monarch amongst this rabble. Since I asked first, you shall present first!"

When the sun had dared peek its radiant face over the eastern horizon that morning, Bort had suspected that it would be a particularly splendid day. When the clouds had failed to coalesce and conceal the lustrous rays, and when the northern breeze had charged into the city like an invading army robbing the place of its stickiness and humidity, it was clear that something truly notable was afoot. But it was not until the portent of the unfinished lentil soup had transpired that Bort was certain that this day would herald a grand march for the freelance rhymer. So it was to come in this form?

Clearing his throat and clutching his threadbare tunic, he assumed his stance. And with a melodic tenor voice as clear as the morning, he sang out:

Throb in my back ache!

Thumbtacks in the dell!

Hope springs forth eternal,

Tumbling down to Hell.

Weebles wobble nightly

Though sinners never weep,

Kick the sand so slightly

Then kick a chimney sweep.

Throw him down the stairwell,

Chuck him in the soup,

Mix in all the veggies

Then cover him with goop.

Planting ripe tomatoes

Can be a sorry sight:

They tend to fall on pavement

And never come up ripe.

The roar of applause was thunderous if not deafening. In that moment, Bort knew with certainty that he had achieved his ultimate rhyming goal: he had entertained and pleased all of his spiritual subjects. The expressions of delight on their ignoble unwashed faces were universal and undeniable; he had touched a chord amongst them, and Arjazet stood no chance of matching, let alone surpassing, his dispatch, despite the countenance of condescending puzzlement that she projected now.

Bort allowed himself the briefest moment of hubris. For once, failing to marshall his pride and practise some degree of restraint, he allotted himself a tight grin lasting no more than half a heartbeat, but surely not missed by the patiently watching princess. Bort's heart iced with her cold glance, and her eyes continued to burn into his shamed soul for another second. Then she mercifully looked away. Bort's rejoicing was at an end.

Arjazet stepped forward, waited for the applause to die down, waited a few moments longer for dramatic effect, then launched into her tale. Like a thunderclap, she brought her two hands together above her head. Her face twisted in visual locution, seeming to redden and lengthen. A new voice erupted from the geologic fissure that had been her mouth. It murmured then ripened to a roar.

She hissed and purred, twittered and projected. Where Bort would have thrust into the narrative with a vengeance, she exuded such sly and quixotic subtlety that the ear was bathed in allegory. With stick-like animation, her whole body spoke the indirect story. Arjazet wove a fine and layered tapestry of symbol upon sign, calling forth the deepest subconscious hooks that lay buried beneath the human literary psyche. No learned scholar could doubt that she was indeed the master storyteller she claimed to be.

With every phrase, with each nuance of gesture and each twitch of a facial muscle, Bort fell further into despair. Not even he could deny his challenger's talent. It was immense. Had the morning sun lied? It seemed so; this might not be the day of glory he had foreseen. He cringed at a vision: that of having to bow his head before this vile road princess whenever she passed.

Arjazet finished her sophisticated tale, pausing once more to allow the high ideals of her tale's moral to be digested, then returned to her normal stance. Her tangled face was restored to its pale neutrality, her heaving chest barely noticeable beneath the asexual gown. And she waited. And waited.

Finally, from the back, a pair of hands were brought together in applause. Neighbours were reluctantly infected, and they, too, offered soft salvos. Gradually, a smattering of polite clapping peaked with a whistle or two. But there was no more.

Bort had won.

The storyteller's eyes were quiet. She had delivered perhaps the finest performance she was capable of, and it had not been enough. And yet her stolid features betrayed no extreme anguish, nor anger, nor vengefulness.

The mendicants of the street are a discerning lot, though, and to them her reaction was obvious and unmistakable: she was clearly crushed. But she accepted defeat admirably, even bowing deeply before the undisputed champion. How to interpret her blankness but as a mien of confusion? Bort studied her carefully, finally locating the burning spirit of profound disappointment hidden behind her eyes. "Don't you see," he said, searching for the explanation whilst giving it, "you've got to know your audience."

There was further silence between them, but it was not awkward. The urchins began to bore of the exchange, and many quickly frittered away. "With these two baubles," Bort said, fondling the marble and the counterfeit coin, "perhaps we could manage to share a bowl of lentil soup?"

Arjazet blinked neutrally. The philosopher king and queen of the street set off to enjoy their royal lunch.

On Germ Warfare and Bad Sex

JULY 8, approximately 7:34 AM Greenwich Mean Time.

Klaus Hermann, physicist at large, drives his Volkswagen convertible along a Mannheim freeway. The road is flat, unchanging, and the skyline is uniform. The zipping lane markers create a subtle state of psychosis within his expanding brain, and things begin to happen. It comes to him: the Unified Field Theorem, the one simple equation that forms order from chaos, links quantum mechanics with gravity, and adds meaning to the Universe as a whole.

Hermann reaches over to his glove compartment for a note-pad, his palms sweaty with excitement. He then promptly dies as his car hits the guard rail.

*

"Mr President, if we hit Irkutz first, then somehow blame the Chinese, we could create true chaos in an otherwise distressingly stable zone." General Gronski beams over his boss, smiling with satisfaction. Discord is his *raison d'tre*.

The President frowns. "I don't know. Is it possible?"

"What about germs, Sir?" First Secretary Jamieson interrupts, quite loud in his exuberance. "We've spent millions on bio-research, so let's use it, eh? We'll have to implement them germs someday, you know. Treasury tells me we're wasting billions in storing 'em."

"There is that."

"But Irkutz, Mr President! We haven't had a satisfying covert experience in decades!"

"This is true," The President nods thoughtfully. "But the Russians are our friends now."

"What better time to shake them up?"

"Germs, Sir, that's where the future is. Nukes are pass . If we have to take Irkutz, let's do it with germs. American troops are American troops, no matter how small they are . . ."

The President stands, raising his elected arms to signal a ceasefire. "Gentlemen, I've made a decision." Silent anticipation. "Let's set up a committee to look into it." *Smileunt Omnes*. "So, ah, let's order lunch, okay?"

*

Charles Winfield marches up to the podium, still slightly tipsy after the eggnog he has had for breakfast. He looks out into the sea of eager eyes: multisexed, multiracial, multiplicable multi what? Oh, too much eggnog . . .

"Today," he begins, pausing deliberately because in his notes is written in boldface: PAUSE. "Today my topic is orgasm."

*

Jan Xing sits in the lotus position, swaying back and forth, letting his soul mingle with the poignant scents of the burning incense logs; letting his essence wander along the valley; letting mind and spirit bond in a realm beyond the physical. The Himalayan winds whip his decades-old beard into a vicious frenzy, further drying his cratered and desertlike face.

"Let's have a little magic. Where's the magic . . . Let's have a little magic," he mutters to no one.

The holy mists coalesce around him, clinging to him like adoring idolaters, giving him a puffy, somewhat humorous appearance.

Yet no one laughs, for Jan Xing is alone on his mountain, alone with his God.

*

"But nobody lives in Irkutz, Mr President, only Russians!"

"We shall see, General Gronski, we shall see."

"I have some pictures of germs here . . ." Jamieson rummages in his case. "Here. Look at this beauty, Sir: *Eschereschi Bocculae*. Look at them curves. Kills in minutes . . ."

"Mr President," Gronski cuts in, "we've had nukes for, what, fifty years now? And I ask you: have we ever used 'em? I mean, except for the first two times? They're rotting in the silos, becoming unsafe and unreliable. We can't disassemble them, there's too much waste . . ."

"Now this baby here," Jamieson resumes his rummaging, "Name's *Corundum Bubonus*. The lab boys call her the 'Yellow Death'. Cute, eh? 'Yellow Death'. Makes good print."

The President stands, parting his staff in practised Moses-like fashion. "Gentlemen, I've come to a decision." He looks around, marshalling his considerable charm. "I'll have the lobster."

*

Jan Xing extends his awareness: past the valley, beyond the mountain range itself. He is in a small Indian village, in the home of one Bindu Nandlall, Brahmin at large.

Jan Xing absorbs his environment, taking it all in. He observes Bindu Nandlall sitting on the floor in the corner, eating something out of a small clay bowl. Smells like rice.

Nandlall looks at Jan Xing's magically coalescing form, shrugs, then steps out to visit the latrine. Best way to deal with ghosts is always a good piss.

*

"Over the years orgasm has become something of a mystery. No one is ever quite sure if they have indeed experienced it. Nor is this corruption a recent one. I have uncovered incontestable proof that there exists, right here in our country, a highly placed right-wing conspiracy to abolish true orgasm."

Sudden shocked intakes of breath from the crowd.

"And the Grand Dragon of this well-concealed plot is none other than our own beloved President!"

*

"This lobster is damned good!" exclaims the American chief. (Jamieson quickly scribbles this statement into his notes. Upon his retirement he intends to publish *Famous Presidential Quotations* and become rich.)

"Now the way I see it," Gronski says, "we can arrange to send a peace-keeping force to Irkutz . . ."

The President almost chokes. "It's in fucking Russia!" (Jamieson does not write this down.) "Excuse my French."

"But you see, Sir, after we bomb it, it'll be on the moon!" Gronski is never one for tasteful humour, but usually gets away with blaming it on years of military conditioning. He sits back, quite satisfied with himself. He seriously considers ordering a second lunch, his brain urgently demanding nourishment after his exhausting cerebral display.

"You know," Jamieson muses. "Each soldier could carry a vial of *Corundum Bubonus* in his mouth, or in other body cavities . . ."

"What's this here?" the President asks, glaring suspiciously at one of Jamieson's bacterial micrographs.

"Oh, that one's still experimental, too nasty even for us to use. It's called *Extremus Impotentus*. Supposed to permanently impair the male body's ability to achieve orgasm."

The President's eyes take on a distant, glazed-over look.

*

The rice isn't bad, Jan Xing thinks to himself. Bindu Nandlall returns to the hut, carrying his four-month-old son. The child is remarkably unattractive; even the household's animals seem dismayed by his repugnant features.

Jan Xing frowns with disapproval, then reflects embarrassingly on his own lack of physical appeal.

He etiolates out of view, taking the ethereal path back to his lofty perch in the Himalayas.

*

BEEP BEEP BEEP. "Yah, what is it? The President is having lunch."

"Sorry to interrupt, Mr Jamieson, but there have been some interesting developments. We must speak to the President."

"Go on," the President says, wiping lobster juice from his chin.

"Sir, the Russians have bombed New York."

"Nukes?" Gronski cuts in.

"No, sir. Germs."

'I knew it!" Jamieson leaps to his feet, an exultant Archimedean look enshrined on his chiselled face.

The voice from the cellular phone continues: "Orders, Mr President?"

"Get ready to launch everything we've got. Germs, too. And have Edna express my condolences to the families of those killed. That should keep her busy for a while."

*

"To quote an unnamed philosopher: 'Is it ejaculation, or is it orgasm? Is it an involuntary pelvic contraction, or is it orgasm?' And that," concludes Charles Winfield, "is my theory on the rapidly declining rate of orgasm in the United States of America."

The roar of applause, the shrieks of adulation and of shock. Charles Winfield is a hero and a crusader. Charles Winfield is a true American, in the finest sense of that particular tiresome compliment.

Charles Winfield and his entire audience are then vaporized as a commie nuke climaxes one mile above the amphitheatre.

*

To say that Jan Xing is surprised to find his body missing would be an understatement. People just don't go about stealing other people's bodies when they've temporarily vacated them. Especially when this particular body is high up on a mountain.

When Jan Xing goes searching for his body, all he finds are charred remains of others, quite unsuitable for occupation. The entire globe, with the exception of one particular Indian village, has been completely sterilized.

Well, he muses, life is never boring.

*

It is some time later, after all the disembodied souls have had time to become acquainted with their new mode of existence, that the entity that was once called Charles Winfield meets up with a foreigner.

"Hi, I'm Klaus Hermann, physicist at large."

"Do you experience orgasm?"

"There was something important I want to tell everyone, but I can never remember what it was. It is perpetually poised on the edge of my tongue, but never manages to alight. You understand?"

"Sort of like unsatisfying sex."

"Well," Hermann sighs dejectedly, "perhaps someday I shall remember what it was."

*

It is about that time that Aaron Nandlall, Bindu's ugly infant son, gets hold of his father's pencil and scribbles some gibberish on the bottom of the clay bowl from which Bindu usually eats his rice. The characters bear a peculiar resemblance to Indo-Arabic numerals, and the overall scribble is slightly reminiscent of what other people might be inclined to call the Unified Field Theorem.

But Aaron drops the bowl, it shatters, and Bindu throws it away.

Aaron Nandlall grows up to be a cowherd, though, and he never thinks twice about it.

The Reef

THE WATER seemed to glisten that evening. There was less foam on the surface, and there were fewer bubbles rising from the recesses of the dark coral. But it was more than that. The starlight seemed to filter all the way down to the seabed from the heavens, spicing the brine water and lending it a sparkling sweet taste.

Milanario treaded quietly a few metres below the surface, moving just enough to keep warm. Somewhere, not too far off, her little sister Thecantra was searching for gilabeek eggs.

It was a good night for finding gilabeek eggs. The little blue and white fish preferred moonless nights like this one for depositing their delicious eggs in the nooks and crannies of the coral reef. But, contrary to her original plans, Milanario didn't feel quite like hunting down the precious stashes.

Her spine tingled as tiny water currents caressed the webbing between her toes, and the periodic warm water from the coral bed rose to wash over her shivering slick torso.

What was it about this night? It was the shortest night of the year, the astronomers had said, with a rare conformation in which none of the three major moons were visible. But that would have nothing to do with the water, except for the tides. And the reef felt so wonderfully static for a dynamic community!

A jet of cold current on her left side announced the return of Thecantra. The little one paddled up alongside her older sister, a cluster of sticky pink eggs clutched in one hand.

"Want one?" She signalled with her free hand.

"No, thank you, Thecantra. You can have them all." Milanario signalled back, quite lethargically.

Thecantra's brow furrowed, and her semiformed face looked profoundly confused. "But you always eat gilabeek eggs!"

"Not this time. I'm not hungry."

Thecantra shrugged and popped a pink ovule into her salivating mouth. Milanario raised an index finger and jabbed it up in the signal for "surface." Thecantra nodded and followed her up and into the night air.

Breaking the calm of the surface, Milanario took several deep breaths, replenishing her lungs and returning the colour of her skin to normal. Once, as a child, she had forgotten to refill her lungs and had turned a bright blue. Mother had had to drag her to the surface before she succumbed to hypoxia. As a result, she kept a close watch over Thecantra's hue, while consciously fighting her maternal instincts.

As they lingered on the surface, Milanario took great efforts to disturb the surface as little as possible, becoming mildly distressed when Thecantra decided to paddle about furiously. There was an almost hypnotic quality to the water's stillness, and Thecantra's movements were certainly out of place within the unmoving portrait of aquatic placidity.

"Milanario," Thecantra said. "Why is this called John Addams's World?"

"Because John Addams discovered it, stupid."

"Who was here before him?"

"Nobody. Just the coral reef and a few of the octopi. You'll learn about all that in school."

"Where did the gilabeek fish come from?"

"I said you'll learn about that in school!"

Thecantra pouted and looked away. Never had Milanario ever encountered a child so eager to go to school. The little pest would spend the rest of her childhood trying the think up ways to avoid it, though!

"The first colonists brought the gilabeek and the other fish from Urth fifteen thousand years ago."

"Oh." She seemed happy again. A small price to pay, Milanario thought, to keep the runt manageable.

The moonless sky was soul-chilling. A million billion distant suns beat down on them, but only flickers were perceptible: a million billion tiny fires burning in the sky. And, where the sky met the sea on a liquid horizon, only a subtle difference between the two was perceptible.

Strangely, the water surface remained motionless except for the occasional fish that would leap skyward for either a gasp of air or a mouthful of bugs and, of course, for Thecantra's endless paddling about.

The shore was almost invisible, too, which was surprising since it was only about half a kilometre away. If it were not for the tall frawn trees blocking out the star field here and there, the land would have been undetectable.

Milanario found comfort in the semiblackness. The odd juxtaposition of cool air with the illusion of warmth soaked in from the salty water, and the caress of gentle eddies against her relaxed body, were mere unconscious niceties. But the darkness of the night, tempered by the subtle glow of the distant horizon, and the slight white noise of shifting waters and a billowing breeze were a sensory throwback to long-buried memories of the womb.

She was once more a babe afloat in a bag of sweet prenatal fluids.

"Milanario?"

"Yes? What is it now?"

"How come everything's so weird?"

She felt it, too! So it wasn't imagination after all. It wasn't what mother would have called the "romantic meanderings of adolescent minds," triggered by unusual astronomical conformations and plentiful gilabeek eggs. It was a real, tangible difference in the environment!

"How so, Thecantra?" She strained to conceal her excitement. Her sister would deliver a more truthful response this way.

"You know what I mean! There're no moons, but it's still bright. And the water's colder in some parts, and hot in others. And the whole place seems kind of quiet. And the gilabeek eggs are kind of sour. And the coral bed is making weird sounds . . ."

"What?!"

"Yup! Right about where I found the eggs, the reef was kind of groaning!"

"Show me!"

Without responding, Thecantra pulled her knees to her chest, tipped her head downward, and pushed off for the seabed once again. Milanario followed with gentle kicks from her webbed feet.

As they descended, their blurred blue field of vision was gradually replaced by the craggy outline of the majestic coral reef, the largest indigenous community on John Addams's World. Entire schools of multicoloured fish seemed to oscillate with a singleness of mind no poet could adequately describe, nor any scientist explain.

Milanario's experienced eye detected snatches of darting bright orange and red flesh: the rare appearances of juranui and parrot fish whose dazzling colouration betrayed the poison in their bloodstreams or rather the emulation of truly poisonous creatures, for the original colonists had taken great pains to avoid importing dangerous fauna. The colonists had been, however, only partly successful, as some predacious creatures lingered still further out in the ocean.

The sisters' bodies arced softly in a pleasing trajectory, gently skimming over the coral heads with a precision of control challenged only by the permanent coral residents. As Thecantra's hand began to dip down to touch a coral head, Milanario snatched it up with her own.

"Don't touch the tentacles!" She signalled to her baby sister.

"Why not?"

"The soft ones exude a lytic poison which would dissolve your flesh!" Her choice of exotic words impressed upon her sister the import of her warning. Thecantra seemed to turn pale, but in the water it was difficult to tell. Milanario was exaggerating, of course, as one must do when cautioning Thecantra. But the lytic poison certainly would have stung, and Milanario would have had to nurse a crying baby back to shore. And that would have been a waste of a truly exceptional evening.

After all, she had worked so hard to escape her evening studies. With the batting of adolescent eyelids and her insistence on the importance of the evening swim and the hunt for gilabeek eggs so much so that one would have thought the end of the world was near she had coerced Mother to let her and Thecantra go. The latter's presence was always a condition, the burden of an elder sister, as if in her mother's mind Thecantra's presence would somehow deter Milanario from exploring to the full extent of her adventurous heart's desire.

Though loathe to admit it publicly, or indeed consciously, somehow Milanario couldn't imagine truly enjoying an activity without Thecantra. She was addictive, in her own annoying way.

"Here!" Thecantra indicated a patch of coral head no different from the others. There was no doubt of the location, however, for her sense of direction and short memory were quite good for her age.

Milanario lowered her ear to the coral head, careful not to touch the outstretched tendrils.

"I don't hear anything."

"Try harder!"

"Thecantra, there's no sound here. You must have been mistaken."

It was rather sad, actually. Milanario had been hoping for some tangible physical manifestation even something as elusive as a strange sound to anchor this night of altered perceptions in her memory. She searched desperately for a noise, any noise, but despite herself heard nothing.

Thecantra floated down to place her own ear next to the coral head. "It's gone now," she signalled. "It was like a moaning. I didn't imagine it!"

"I didn't say that you did . . ."

"But you thought it!"

Milanario treaded silently as her little sister puttered around trying to find the strange sound. It was so peaceful down here, so static. Yet this mystery had lent the environment a welcome tingling sensation, an excitement of sorts. It was such a pleasing experience that Milanario lost track of the time. Thecantra was still a relatively healthy shade of pink, though, so there was no immediate need to return to the surface.

The astronomer named Stonn was always of a bluish hue, even when he was out of the water. When he swam with Mother, she never seemed at ease, as if she were afraid she'd have to rescue Stonn at any moment.

This had always seemed to Milanario to be another of Mother's paranoid excesses. After all, no human had drowned on John Addams's World for as long as Milanario could remember not unless something had trapped him beneath the surface, or he had been knocked unconscious by a clumsy whale or giant octopus.

Back on Urth, they say, drownings were so common that many people never ever went into the water. However did they avoid shrivelling up beneath the sun's heat?

Stonn had been at their family's domicile just as the sisters were leaving for their swim. He had seemed agitated and excitable but then he was always excited about something. Perhaps that was why Mother loved him so. Stonn certainly displayed the appropriate filial qualities to elicit great affection from Mother.

"Milanario," Thecantra signalled, jolting her sister from her shallow reverie.

"Yes?"

"Where have all the fish gone?"

Indeed, the oscillating schools were nowhere to be seen. They had been there a moment ago. Or was it an hour ago? Had they drifted? But the same coral heads were beneath them, and the coral does not drift does it? Milanario was terribly confused.

But she dared not show any sign of fear to her baby sister. Not only would it impart further fear on the little one, it would also be horribly embarrassing!

"They've probably found a richer food source elsewhere. This region has little plankton."

"Over there!" Thecantra pointed in the direction of the waiting ocean. Sure enough, there were flickers of multicoloured fish and phospho-luminescent crustaceans. The schools had, indeed, moved further out. "Let's go see!"

"Thecantra, wait!" But she was already gone. All Milanario could do was tag along behind.

The water was very much darker here. Perhaps they were beneath an overhang of an uncharted island or peninsula. More probably, there were clouds in the sky preventing starlight from diffusing down. Milanario's hand struck something hard, a crustacean of sorts. She glanced over to discover that she had inadvertently captured a lamp crab whose internal luminescence would provide her with light.

Holding the crab to her face, she rediscovered the water. The blackness was perforated with specks of white where the light reflected off floating particles. It seemed the black ocean of space, with all its twinkling stars, had been recreated down here in the real ocean. An underwater astronomer's delight!

But where was Thecantra?

"Thecantra!" She signalled, now somewhat frightened. But, of course, there was no response as Thecantra could not possibly see her hands in the blackness. Quite against her natural tendencies, Milanario acted out of desperation. She released a mouthful of her precious lung air into the water, allowing a loud *GALUMP*! to accompany its liberation.

Almost instantly, the yellow-pink cherubic face of her ward appeared in the lamp crab's field of luminosity. Milanario struggled to conceal her sigh of relief.

"Plankton!" Thecantra signalled. "Lots of it!"

Milanario frowned. The particles looked like plankton, but they were unlike any plankton she had ever seen before. And the fish were not gobbling it up as quickly as they would devour normal plankton.

Memories of primary school chemistry stirred in the recesses of Milanario's mind, including visions of taste tests and the merits of saliva. She had read that such methods did not exist back on Urth, but were an entirely new science developed on John Addams's World.

Just how different were her distant Urth ancestors? Could they not see the obvious simplicity and accuracy of taste analysis? And was there any truth to the belief that they could only hold their breaths for a few minutes at a time . . .?

In a moment of impetuousness and, perhaps, foolhardiness, she stretched out her neck, opened her mouth, and took in a gulp of the strange plankton.

She swished it about with her tongue experimentally, allowing it to mix completely with her saliva. The strange taste betrayed the substance's alien nature. Violently, Milanario spewed her mouthful back into the ocean, rinsing her mouth out further with the welcome brine water.

It wasn't plankton.

What was it?

Thecantra had watched the entire experiment in horror. But she had been too fascinated and too confident in Milanario to object. She was alert enough, however, to perceive her sister's conclusion: If it wasn't natural plankton, where had it come from?

"Excrement from a passing giant octopus?"

Milanario made a face of disgust in response. "I don't think so, Thecantra. The giant octopi don't come in this close."

Following Milanario's lead, the pair swam further out into the heart of the particle cloud. Its increasing density was an illusion, they discovered, created by the extensiveness of the cloud. It seemed to be of a consistent distribution throughout. Milanario's skin bristled as they penetrated the cloud, and she fought a slight but annoying tingling at the base of her spine. Certain primal responses, it seemed, were stirring within her. But the non-plankton could not be responsible. It just floated along like so much microscopic debris.

The fish did not eat of it, nor did the non-plankton seem to be doing anything. But the particles did seem to be drifting slowly downward, even though there was no deposit of them on the ocean floor.

"Milanario?"

"Yes?" She signalled back expectantly, worried that Thecantra had come upon some sort of danger.

"How long has the coral reef been here?" Milanario sighed inwardly. *It's only one of her silly, limitless questions.*

"No one knows. Remember that I said it was here when the original colonists arrived?"

"Has it always been this big?"

Milanario paused. A question she could not answer! "I don't know, Thecantra. I guess I've always assumed that it has always girdled the continent."

"And the other continent?"

"No one lives there. It's much too hot."

"No, but is there coral there, too?"

"I don't know. The astronomers would know, I think. Stonn would probably know."

"Let's go ask him!"

"No." She didn't give a reason. She didn't have to. Thecantra would always obey her, despite her complaining. Besides, the reason, she hoped, was quite obvious: to return to shore now would ruin the night's experience.

Hypnotically, the ever-present reef fish oscillated in unison beneath her. It seemed that no matter what the immediate environment, these lovely little creatures could always be found engaged in their bizarre and ancient dance. How Milanario longed to understand them, to join in their primal cotillion. It was impossible, she felt, to witness the underwater ballet and fail to be drawn strangely to the unexplained community consciousness.

Suddenly Thecantra dipped her nose downward and paddled furiously. She sped past Milanario, caressing the latter's body with a warm jet stream. Milanario spun in three dimensions, frantically trying to locate her sister in the blackness.

Stillness.

Where could she have gone and why?

The ocean darkened. Not even the illuminated non-plankton, nor the reef bed below, emanated light. The darkness enclosed about Milanario, pushing her farther from Thecantra, and farther from shore. The warm, comfortable water seemed now to be frigid and dangerous. Where was Thecantra?!

A hand grasped her wrist, and Milanario stiffened.

"Thecantra! Where did you go?"

"Quickly! Follow me!" She signalled back.

"Why . . . ?" But Thecantra was pulling her down towards the reef, pushing her face towards the deeper ocean. Then Milanario saw it: a family of sharks, barreling directly towards them at full tilt.

Milanario froze, but just for a moment. Then she was off at full speed too, betraying the athletic ability that had lain dormant in her floating body for many hours. Easily, she overtook Thecantra, then dragged the younger one behind her. They would make it to the crags of the reef in time but then what?

Like a creature of the reef, Milanario arced her body at precisely the right angle, deftly avoiding the searching tendrils while positioning herself and Thecantra inside a coral hole, a living cave.

Despite the fear, the knowledge of impending doom, and the immense rush of adrenaline clouding her mind, Milanario retained enough conscious thought to wonder, What were sharks doing so near the reefs? There were "reef sharks" back on Urth, she had been told, but they had not been brought to John Addams's World. The sharks here had never before dared to venture so close to the poisonous coral heads.

As if on cue, a deathly piscine grin presented itself immediately above them, its pointed teeth resembling the harpoons that the fishermen wielded to kill frightened fish so efficiently.

Thecantra opened her mouth in a silent scream, and a bit of air escaped from her lungs. Though she and her sister were still not blue, Milanario was concerned for their oxygen debt. The sharks could keep them pinned here for hours. But Thecantra could not hold her breath for nearly that long. And Milanario probably would not last much longer, either.

Lacing her fingers tightly around her little sister's upper arm, Milanario kicked lightly away from the prowling shark, being careful to keep a coral head between it and them. The shark did not seem to recognize the toxicity of the waving tendrils did it not know?

The game continued for what seemed like hours, but was more like minutes. Milanario deftly maintained their position of safety within the reef's comforting embrace, while the predators were locked out. Never before had she felt so much like a denizen of the reef, exercising a solidarity with the other inhabitants who were also hiding from the sharks.

But it was a solidarity in intent alone, for she was wholly unable to improve the lot of the other reef creatures, nor could they offer her any assistance. She could only watch in horror as entire schools of dancing reef fish were gobbled up by the intruders, rudely aware that their watery ballet had ended prematurely.

Meanwhile, Thecantra had discovered something new. The coral was moaning again. Presently, Milanario felt it, too. Even the sharks seemed to pause in their task as the low grumbling shook their bodies. Then, strangest of all, they saw that in unison with the rhythmic rumbling, the coral heads were exuding a powdery substance: the alien non-plankton.

The powdery clouds belched forth from the coral heads, expanding in white spheres of rapidly dissipating consistency. And where they intersected with groups of fish, a brief frenzy would ensue, soon to be replaced by a calmness broken only by the threat of the interloping predators.

Milanario, too, could feel a quickening in her blood that coincided with the rumblings of the reef cave that shielded her. Thecantra did not seem as affected, and Milanario had to wonder if the sensations were nothing more than terror mixed with worry and physical stress.

In moments of extreme danger, it is said, the sentient brain will cogitate on matters of less immediate importance, but of lasting conceptual gravity. And so it was with Milanario who, while sharks struggled ferociously to devour her and her sister, suddenly became aware of the "grand unity of all things." The strange misgivings she had experienced the result of subtle biochemical changes within her body? To what end, and from what stimulus? The quiet of the ocean, the eerie luminescence of the watery beds, and the appearance of sharks this far in, added to the primal thumpings of the ancient coral and its excretion of the non-plankton, summed to a complex biological intermingling across several subtle media.

But why? And how was the rare astronomical conformation connected?

Glistening daggers of enamel jutted towards her, as a large male shark attempted to poke his head between coral heads. Again, Milanario and Thecantra screamed underwater, feeling the sound waves pulsate through the reef and expand outward at a high velocity. The quiet of the ocean had been replaced with a deafening orgy of violence.

Milanario kicked harder, pulling Thecantra along a narrowing groove of the reef bed. The coral heads were denser here, and they risked being stung. But the tendrils almost always waved away from the reef, towards potential attackers. Thus, the pursuing shark was stung repeatedly, causing him to writhe in considerable pain. He jetted off, unhurt. But he would return when his ego was soothed and his appetite remained unsated. The other members of his pack did not learn by his example, however, and soon were bearing down upon the trapped and weary pair.

The exertion had shortened Milanario's path to oxygen debt, and she was feeling the first twinges of respiratory discomfort. Ordinarily, this would be the ideal time to head for the surface for a replenishing breath of night air. But circumstances prevented this action.

Thecantra, while not as aerobically worked as her older sister, was still distressed. Her normal pink hue was now a neutral pale white. When the first blue specks appeared, irreversible nervous damage would not be far away.

Their time was short.

Milanario's grip on Thecantra's forearm loosened, and her full attention was put into controlling her breathing reflex. She must remain calm, conserve energy and thus oxygen. This was the only way. But it would not be enough, she realized. The sharks would not leave for some time; this was much too promising a feeding ground for them.

She felt consciousness slipping away. Good training and good genes kept her from reflexively breathing in a lungfull of water. But it was only a matter of time. She felt herself being pulled by the currents from her sanctuary in the reef's groove, out into the open water, and lacked the strength to resist.

Her vision had reduced to a long dark tunnel with fuzzy edges and a thumping headache to match. A lifeless doll, she hung in the centre of one of the expanding spheres of non-plankton, feeling the warmish eddies lap at her sides while the unknown powder seeped into her nostrils and caked somewhat upon her feet's webbing.

There was movement around her, she could tell, but her eyes could not focus on anything except a distant point of radiance that seemed to grow brighter as the expanding bubble pushed her up, forcing her to the surface atop a parabolic waveform.

And where were the daggerlike teeth that were no doubt searching out her young flesh? Had they already devoured half of her, leaving her nervous system unable to detect the loss? There was, after all, no feeling, no perception of any kind except a desperate clutch on consciousness and an eerie blue glow that filled her eyes.

Her lungs could be restrained no longer. Her throat and rib muscles finally recoiled, allowing her chest to collapse, forcing out the expended air, then expanding to be filled . . .

Thecantra . . . ?!

And cold night air struck her in the face, triggering her breathing reflex further. She gave in and enjoyed the infusion of large breaths of very welcome dry air. Thecantra was beside her, she knew, also breathing well. Neither of them showed any lasting ill effects from oxygen deprivation, only an understandable disorientation and fatigue.

"The sharks," Thecantra said, no longer dependent on their underwater hand language. "Where are they?"

Milanario dropped several metres below the surface to look around. The sharks were there, as were the other reef fish. But they, too, were caught up in the frenzy of the expanding bubbles of non-plankton. The situation was temporary, she reasoned from their own experiences, and surely their attackers would shortly be once more fully in control of their own faculties and still in search of a meal.

"We have to hurry home, Thecantra." But her sister gazed longingly at her. She clearly lacked the strength to do anything more than tread water.

Milanario cast her gaze once more toward the shore, where the swaying frawn trees still carved out a ghostly sillhouette from the starry night sky. But the horizon's bluish glow had lessened somewhat, and a familiar play of lights in the extreme distance told Milanario that one of the moons would soon be rising, followed at length by the eventual sunrise that would bring to an end this remarkable evening.

What exactly had happened?

As she surveyed the shoreline, trying to regain full control over her eyes, washing the tunnel vision and the bluish haze from her memory, two figures emerged onto the panoply.

"Sharks!" Thecantra cried.

"No," Milanario said. "They're people." The figures approached with majestic silent grace, arcing in and out of the water, dolphin-diving with a rhythmic precision that was almost sexual. The night's strange glow reflected off their naked bodies, glinting at times against something metallic carried by one of the figures.

The sisters watched with a shared admiration for a sight so unexpectedly beautiful. If it were not for the difficult melange of fatigue, stress and fear that had assaulted them in recent minutes, the joy of this vision would have been almost palpable.

It was said that on Urth people had learned to fly. Milanario had often wondered at the spectacle of such a thing and had silently wished that her culture would seek to reclaim the commonplace of that ability, if only for the occasional sight of a human being soaring across the sky's panorama, revelling in the complexity and wonders of his world.

Yet thus was this hypnotic vision, like a drug-driven mirage that teases the optic nerve and washes the soul with hopes and thoughts that blur the line between body and spirit. So striking was the effect on Milanario that she had to gasp when it became clear that the lean muscular body of the lead swimmer was of a bluish hue, despite the erie light that tried to mask its nature. *Stonn*!

"Hello, Milanario. Are you all right?"

"Yes, thank you. Mother, how did you find us?"

"Your screams carried all the way to the village. Stonn triangulated your position."

"There are sharks . . ." Milanario started to say, but Stonn, carrying something, dove beneath the surface.

"It's all right," Mother said. "We brought a pheromonal repellent."

Milanario was bursting to tell her mother all about the strange events of the evening, especially about the amazing non-plankton. But where to start?

"I'm glad we found you," Stonn said, resurfacing. "It is somewhat unsafe to be in the water on this night, although the reef's summoning is hard to resist."

"The what?"

"Have you not noticed the spores floating in the water, Milanario?" Stonn asked.

"Spores?!"

"Indeed. Apparently, every fifteen thousand years or so, signalled by this unusual conformation of the suns and moons, the coral reef reproduces itself. The particles that look like plankton are its spores."

Milanario was overwhelmed. At last, there were answers forthcoming. Yet somehow, the mystery had been more exciting when unexplained. It was as though she had been rudely awakened from a pleasant dream, sharks notwithstanding, dragged unwillingly from an exciting world of strange colours and opiates. She sighed. "You said that the reef summons us," she said.

"Yes. At the time of spawning, it seems, the reef exudes pheromones into the water and air, drawing all its denizens to it, so that all might partake of the fertility fest."

"But we're not indigenous! How can it affect us?"

Her mother smiled and took on a thoughtful expression. "We're all creatures of the reef now, Milanario, forever intertwined with its interests linked to ours. It offers protection to all its inhabitants, as we must protect it." She paused and whispered the last: "John Addams's World has accepted us."

And somehow that made Milanario strangely happy. She had, it seemed, joined in the dance of the reef fish, meditated on the thoughts of the solitary giant octopi, and partaken of the hospitality of the reef. Indeed, she had come to a conclusion of considerable conceptual gravity.

And Thecantra was fast asleep in her mother's arms now, her webbed feet paddling away absently, no doubt driven by some pleasant underwater dream.

El Dorado

YES, THERE probably are fundamentally evil people on this Earth, but I don't think Dr Munroe was one of them. Admittedly, he did appear to be callous and cruel hearted at times, but that was just his way a need to be honest, even in demeanour. What others might construe as rancour, Dr Munroe was more apt to characterize as direct or forthright. And he was nothing if not direct.

His strength, I contend, was his knowledge of self. He was aware of the darkness that seeped within him, as it does within each of us. He, however, was able to give his darkness a name: greed, or avarice. The acknowledgement of his demons, he would argue, is what raised him above the station of most other men. Most of us, at times, have thought some pretty awful thoughts. Don't kid yourself, we've all done it. We give passing nod to the desires and sins that crop up every now and again, then we congratulate ourselves for not having succumbed to those demons. But they still linger. Whatever else has been said of Munroe, at least he kept conscious watch over his demons, sometimes even embracing them.

Dr Munroe was not, I contend, an evil man. His chosen profession, after all, was one that served mankind. Some have insisted that he coveted only the pecuniary advantages of his medical standing, and I cannot disprove this contention. He was, admittedly, quite concerned with the attainment of wealth. But I'd hoped that this was just one of those demons he would acknowledge and eventually conquer.

So that is how his story begins: the quest for wealth.

*

We have all, since earliest childhood, heard the stories of the AmerIndian city of gold, El Dorado. We have been told of the adventurous excursions of Cortez and Pizarro through the jungles of Central and South America, even as far north as Texas, in search of this fabulous fount of precious metal, hidden for millennia beneath the rainforest's living canopy.

We have even heard some talk of the bloody carnage that was coincident with those waves of European treasure-seeking expeditions. A strange thing happens to men when a lure of such purity and immensity is sniffed by that inner darkness; the primal id climbs atop the brain's veneer of reason, and our pretensions to civility are shed like so much thin snake skin. History bears out these failed attempts at monetary glory with, among other things, a drumlin in Guyana named "El Dorado," and books, films and other endless references in popular culture to the fabled city.

History does not, however, allow for many remnants of the destroyed peoples who fell before the wake of this gold lust. As the expeditions pushed further inland, and industrial cities were left to grow on the banks of former tropical lucidity, the fluid tribes who had once melted like shadows into the background of bush and trees vanished for real into a diluted pool of murder and intermarriage. A tragedy, to be sure, considered our Dr Munroe, but one that would not deter him from his quest. Those people were gone, he reasoned, and he could not bring them back. So what harm was there in pursuing their lost city of gold?

He did not think that the colonial Spaniards were necessarily stupid, but the very fact that they had failed to find an entire *city* of solid gold was testament to the inefficiency of their ways. History, again, was rife with detail of Renaissance Spain's technological superiority, especially in their tools of war: the brass that could not be penetrated by Indian arrows, the equestrian tradition that gave them the advantage of four-legged tanks in this lush battlefield. But the stronger is never necessarily the smarter, Munroe once wrote, no doubt remembering bullies of both the schoolyard and the professional world who had tried to impose their wills upon him throughout much of his life.

Munroe's theory was simple: ask the natives where the city was. It was clear that the few remaining Amazonian tribes had no use for gold, other than as a decorative measure. Surely, they had no reason to conceal the city's whereabouts. But, as pointed out by Alphonse, Munroe's guide and translator, the Spaniards had tortured many Central and South Americans several hundred years ago when the knowledge was supposedly fresh and they had turned up nothing!

Ah, Munroe countered, the Spaniards tortured the ignorant citizens of the large Indian cities, not the knowledgeable jungle folk who lived in the trees. It was to that latter group that Munroe would pose his query, and thus obtain from a simple question what generations of armies could not wrest by force.

Alphonse failed to point out to his employer that the native tribes did not, in fact, live in the trees.

*

His arrival in Brazil was uneventful, as was his passage into the jungle. It was more dramatic a change than he had been led to expect, having consulted several Conquistador diaries as references. Back then, the transition from grassland to rainforest was gentle and gradual, so much so that an explorer would begin a journey from the coast, and find himself surrounded by lush walls of vegetation, never having noticed when the change had taken place.

Munroe had looked down from his plane, seeing the effects of the local industry: strip mining and slash-and-burn agriculture. There was a sudden wall of nothingness that marked the boundary between farm and jungle. It certainly made an easy landmark, and it was from this wall that his waterborne expedition would embark.

Munroe and Alphonse paddled down a small unnamed river in a long wooden canoe. Munroe had insisted on a powered boat of some kind but, not knowing much about boating or jungles, had conceded to Alphonse's experienced suggestion that canoe was the best way to traverse the jungle. Initially they paddled for only a few hours a day. Then, as Munroe became more accustomed to the physical exertion, they paddled almost all day and night.

The experience was, as Munroe was later to record in his memoirs, rather surreal. The sounds of the jungle, at first annoying and obtrusive, had melted into the visual spectacle, complementing it. Squawks of strange birds, screeches of arboreal primates, and the frantic splashes of schools of carnivorous fish accentuated the canoers' rhythmic paddling.

In daylight, the sun beat down upon them like the mighty god for which it was once mistaken. The spectrum of technicolour birds washed across the sky, again in a kind of rhythmic cadence, and the occasional small mammal would dart through the trees, just slowly enough that its presence could not be reasonably questioned.

At night, the noises were not as highly pitched, but the insects convened for the silent blood feast. Sounds of supposed caimans sliding across the mud into the river kept them awake, and the regular swarm of fruit bats would block out the moon as the creatures of the night came forth to claim their due.

But, above all this organic distraction, the true appeal of the place was mineral in nature. Alphonse had called it the Amazon's curse. Munroe called it Destiny. It was unmistakable to anyone who spent more than a few days upon the river: its gleam and sparkle. The river's sediment was caked with dissolved gold. Some had theorized that all the Amazonian rivers flowed from El Dorado, so that, in a few thousand years, the city of gold would be entirely washed into the ocean. Others cared not of its source but of its existence. Millions of illegal miners were rumoured to infest the water network, polluting the rivers with smuggled mercury, the cheapest chemical means of extracting the gold.

Real subterranean mines were also rumoured to be scattered throughout the junglescape, most of them abandoned after only a few years of operation: the jungle could be generous, but only for a short time. To minds of a sufficient bent, these rumours pointed hazily towards the existence of a great cache of metallic wealth. Men of great feeling and of inward view are driven by such clues, such insights into mythology and history, it's often been said. These observations were foods of uncertain tastes to Dr Munroe, causing him to smack his lips and to lick the sweat from the sides of his mouth. The rivers were veins of a great organism, he observed, with mineral blood pulsing through them, towards a heart of solid gold.

The sparkling of the river was hypnotic and allowed Munroe to keep on paddling well past his usual physical limits. The hazy vision of a celestial city of soft metal, nestled at the conflux of mighty glistening rivers, was one that sapped the fatigue from his muscles and gave focus and clarity to a mind usually burdened with schemes and designs.

Alphonse, the guide, appeared nonplussed by the watery enhancement, though he found it charming in a passing aesthetic sense. Beneath his breath, though, he cursed the glimmer, exhaling a silent wish for every atom of gold to be replaced by one of carbon or other cheap element.

*

They had spotted alien canoes in the distance on two occasions. Alphonse recognized them as belonging to Yanomami natives but could not communicate with them at a distance. Despite their diligent paddling and newly generated boating endurance, the pair could not catch the sleek Yanomami craft. The Indians seemed to flee as soon as the intruders came into view. Alphonse claimed it was their boat's markings. Munroe had purchased the boat from a river miner. Naturally the Yanomami would run from possible abuse.

On the sixth day riverbound, they finally did make contact with a Yanomami group. It was at a narrowing of the river, so the jungle people could not outpace them without endangering their vessel. They did not, however, seem frightened by the intruders' approach, much to Munroe's surprise. Possibly he had been prepared to use the old "Great White Hunter" ploy that he had seen in so many 1940s American movies. Since he was an urban dweller for whom there is no surviving record of jungle expeditions other than this one, some have theorized that Munroe expected all preindustrial cultures to behave as if Hollywood cameras were pointed at them: to pose nobly yet savagely, and to defer to the technological and intellectual superiority of the better equipped white men.

As they sidled their canoe alongside that of the Yanomami, Munroe took careful stock of the group: a family of two adults, two boys and a girl. The males held bows on their laps, arrows innocently notched and pulled taught. There was no question the arrows were poison-tipped. One thing Munroe had learned of

South America from his medical training was that the deadliest natural poisons were to be tapped from Amazonian plants. He was very conscious of making no misleading hand movements.

"Ask them if they know where El Dorado is," he instructed Alphonse. The translator looked mildly ill, but carried out the request, letting his R's roll a little longer than usual when pronouncing "El Dorado."

Silence.

Then, to the great shock of both Alphonse and Munroe, the male adult pointed south and mumbled something in Yanomami. "He says: 'Follow this river until it intersects another great river. Then follow that river downstream until in ends at a great tree. Walk for three days and nights in the direction pointed by the tree, and you will be at El Dorado.' "

"What does he mean, 'in the direction pointed by the tree'?" Munroe demanded, but the Yanomami craft had pulled away and was making good speed upstream. Alphonse stared at the receding canoe in immobilizing silence for a few moments. Five hundred years of European presence in the New World had not prepared him for the brilliant audacity of this arrogant and naive American doctor.

*

During the voyage they encountered several other Yanomami and Kayapo Indians, each confirming the first's appraisal of El Dorado's location, though none clarifying the "direction pointed by the tree." Munroe's initial shock had worn off and was replaced with a nauseating glow of self-praise. He had been right, and hundreds of Spanish Conquistadors had been wrong.

With every Indian encounter, Munroe had more opportunity to study and, with the few words he managed to pick up, speak with the people. The Kayapo were more warriorlike, he concluded, and had more alien ways than the Yanomami. He found himself liking them best. It was no wonder that a band of Kayapo Indians further up north had forcefully taken a major illegal mining operation on their land and had successfully turned it into a money-making enterprise. Each member of that band was now a millionaire several times over, true testament to the strength and adaptability of Kayapo culture.

"They are now supervising the orderly dismantling of their own rainforest," Alphonse had then commented, according to Munroe's memoirs. But there was no doubt that it took a high degree of effrontery to pull off such an outrageous plan. And such temerity was held in great regard within the swelling heart of the journeying doctor.

Scholars have since pointed to this moment as the opening of Munroe's eyes, the awakening of the feeling human heart within the treasure-seeker's heretofore hollow chest. For, at that moment, he felt regret for his earlier part in an illegal plan to pollute Third World drinking supplies with those neatly packaged French abortion pills. It had seemed, at the time, like a cheap way to control the incredible population explosion in developing areas. But, he was now discovering, even those backward-looking folk with painted faces and loincloths were capable of plans and deeds as "heroic" as his own.

While this was no doubt a major step forward for the very conservative Dr Munroe, there still remained the issue of great wealth to be secured at the end of the quest. Alphonse had been trying, quite unsuccessfully, to explain to him the economic results of his actions. The removal of such a large amount of gold from the region would exacerbate the demise of a hurting regional economy. And if the earlier theories about El Dorado being the source of the rivers' gold sediment were true, he would be impoverishing many millions of river miners.

Munroe bristled at this argument, disdainfully dismissing his guide's liberal hypocrisy. "I thought the river miners were destroying the rivers? Why should you want to protect them?" Alphonse did not answer, but told Munroe of the Indians' claim to the gold of their ancestors. The AmerIndians built the city of gold, he said, why shouldn't their starving descendants inherit it?

"Because if they'd wanted it, they would've gone and gotten it by now. That's why I'm here!" And they paddled on in silence.

*

The jungle sounds weren't as noticeable as before. Perhaps Munroe had become acclimatized to them. Fruit falling from trees were no longer mistaken for noisy caimans sliding into the river. And only a few flocks of multicoloured birds seemed to frequent this area. From farther inland, smells of burning gums and pectins seeped into the travellers' nostrils, locating for them the camp of the rubber tappers far from the riverbed.

After some time, the odour, though dissipating, was giving them headaches. But their weariness permitted them to sleep nonetheless, making them prey to the bad dreams brought by the billowing rubber clouds.

And Munroe dreamt of the city of gold, polished and glistening, with a few snaking vines draped about the idolatrous structures in a sensual caress. There were pyramids of gold, rising to touch the sky, to reach out to the sun god who fed the trees that hid the city. And, hundreds of miles away, the cloud of rubber, methane and charcoal descended on a stampeding herd of cattle.

Ranchers were stealing his gold . . .

The dream then drifted out of reach.

*

Though their heads still hurt slightly from the rubber dreams, they made good time to the end of the second river. It wasn't really an end, as it forked off into two smaller tributary rivers, but at the fork stood the remains of what was once a very large tree.

Alphonse inspected it and, after some time, announced that it had died a couple of years ago. Killed, perhaps, by heavy elements in the water, or by the stench in the air, or by a disease who knew?

But did it still point the way?

No, Alphonse said, not that he could see. Maybe at one time its branches were so arranged that it formed an arrow pointing in a certain direction, but no longer. This was where the quest would end, he said. The Indians' directions depended on this last marker, yet the tribes rarely used these waterways.

"But how would you know?" Munroe accused. "You've never been here, either!" Alphonse was silent. His ruse, as subtle as it had been, had failed. He pointed up to the top of the dead tree. There Munroe saw a tiny living branch a parasitic tree living in the corpse of the great tree. Its sole branch pointed unwaveringly to the northwest, the direction to El Dorado.

"This is where I leave you, Dr Munroe," Alphonse said. "I want none of your gold." Munroe nodded. He didn't need the Brazilian anymore. He had picked up some Spanish, Portuguese and some Yanomami and Kayapo dialects. He could walk for three days along the beaten ground; the jungle was not dense here. When time came for him to go, he would follow the scent of burning pectins to the rubber tappers who would help him.

No, he didn't need Alphonse anymore. And, to himself, he breathed a conceited sigh of relief. The first explorer to reach El Dorado should enter that city alone, borne upon his own feet, and directed by his own solitary dream.

They shook hands and Alphonse paddled away.

*

Munroe's three-day journey on foot was largely uneventful. The ground was soft and quite uneven, causing great fatigue to Munroe's urban form. But his mind, focused on a hazy goal that had taken solid form within his waking dreams, did not allow physical discomfort to slow his trek. The jungle noises had almost ceased altogether, though Munroe still clutched his gun at night. The trees became increasingly sparse as he walked, and more sunlight struck him as the arboreal canopy faded.

The occasional vampire bat would zip by him in the night, its musky smell unmistakable. But what large animal did it prey upon? Surely the ranchers had not encroached this far south.

Eventually he came upon a strip of treeless land, dried and burnt and quite miserable. There were short fragile tree stumps and calcified cow dung aplenty, yet no trees nor cows. He had come upon a failed ranch, now probably the property of a poor farmer who grew about as much food as Munroe himself had grown on his front lawn in downtown Cleveland.

But if a human settlement was once here, why had none of those people found the city of gold?

At the top of a rising, he could see brown smoke billowing from a large invisible source, and vague structures could almost be made out. He climbed the rising tentatively, fearing the worst. As he approached, the sounds of human culture were undeniable: babies crying, dogs barking, meat frying, husbands and wives bickering.

It was a moment of mixed emotions for Munroe. He was thankful for human company after days of loneliness in the jungle, the consuming nature of his vision notwithstanding. At the same time he was soberly aware that his quest had ended.

The mining shanty-town was, of course, called "El Dorado" as a kind of sick joke by its founders. And the occasional Kayapo and Yanomami nomads would come to trade fish and medicine for pots, pans and trinkets. Alphonse had asked the Indians for "El Dorado" and had been directed to El Dorado. Had he asked for "city of gold" well, who knows?

*

Dr Munroe resigned himself to his fate and settled in the miserable little shanty town, where he was genuinely appreciated. With thoughts of French abortion pills behind him, he bent into his new work diligently, treating the sick and poor, and eventually dying sick and poor several years later. A vision of wealth had been successfully replaced by one of usefulness and importance.

But he did find El Dorado. He found the city of gold as the Indians had first described it. It stretched right across Brazil, but was rapidly shrinking. Its gold flowed through its blood, its rivers, in the roots of its trees and in the cells of its animals. At least Dr Munroe had tortured no one for this subtle realization.

And he proved that he was not an evil man.

The Ten Thousand and One Directions

THERE WERE many who believed it was in the British constitution, however unwritten, that the most inhospitable places on Earth were to be second home to the pale effeminate creatures from a wet European isle. How else to explain the deluge of postimperial Raj families in every country with a desert, jungle or snow cap? Or everywhere where bony brown-skinned folk were eager to learn of cricket, parliament, and Oliver Cromwell?

The sun never set on the British empire, but it was truly only a handful of Britons who wandered beyond their small land of bland food, varied ales and inopportune climate. That handful, though, was drawn to ancient places and their tanned races, by reason of exploration, exploitation, or war. Yet it was the latter war that pushed the unadventurous, the homesick, and the bureaucratic to these places heretofore visited only by explorers and scholars.

And it was war that hardened their bodies and softened their perceptions, allowed them to partake of delights and visions that danced on the brink of tangibility. It is said that the denial of comfort and familiarity ripens the brain for infiltration by alien visions and mores. And it is certainly true that times of national and personal insecurity dictate a heightened need for both comfort and familiarity. It is not surprising, then, that the carnage of battle, the spillage of blood, and the wails of heart-rending despair bring forth the subtle in men, as they sink to that common ether of unspoken experience that links us all with that sublime wisdom that is most poignant and sweet upon rolling ocean waves and dry desert sands.

In any case, it was after the Battle of Torch, in which the Vichy French had been routed by the valiant imperial liberators, that the English first encroached upon the poor protectorate of a fellow colonial power. The British had arrived in French Morocco, and even the camels held stiff upper lips.

"Damned dry place, what?" first lieutenant Eric Wilkes was heard to say. Tradition, perhaps, dictated that such things be heard to issue from the mouths of thoughtful commanders. The maintenance of a certain deportment, one simple enough to be mastered by the simplest of men, was imperative. A small populace could spread forth over the entire world if it were borne upon a swift attitude unburdened by the immovability of strong emotion.

It was important, Wilkes felt, to maintain the illusion of dispassion, to deny outsiders purchase on the slippery slope of English fortitude. Or was such insouciance truly illusion? It had been unspoken army policy for so long that he was unsure of its nature: drama or truth. It was a policy, though, that had served him well in India, here in Africa and back home in Yorkshire. In its wisdom, he could see, was the line that separated the ruled from the rulers and the barbarous from the civilized. He could not, then, escape the possibility that his race was somehow naturally reserved, hardened and world-weary. Dispassion came easily to him.

And why not? They were thousands of miles from Yorkshire, where the real war was being fought. Africa was a sideshow. Too bad it was such a damned dry sideshow.

"Yassah!" his sergeant answered robotically.

One more evening with the sultan, perhaps the last. More tradition served as a firm bed upon which Wilkes would comfortably lie. Soon would follow the presentation of gifts, the probing for information, the ingestion of fine foods and wines, and finally the dismissing excuses of tiredness.

For Wilkes this was acceptable, all part of the job. Dispassion and the dictates of civility were painted upon the olive of his uniform, but that paint radiated with diplomatic zeal and the curious slink of the anthropologist. Yet while the simple wine and distinct sultanic foods would coat his innards and briefly hold his longings for Yorkshire at bay, a certain delicate subject must be broached: Wilkes had not seen the alleged thing upon the desert, but could not ignore his man's report.

The desert affected people's brains, this he knew. In daylight, its heat would sap dry the fluids necessary for logical thought, and a certain madness would ensue. At night, the land's endless panorama and biting cold, its shifting footholds and burning stars, would tease the optic nerve and touch that base of primal fear and fantasy that each man keeps buried beneath his calm reverie of reason. This is what he must present to the sultan, not embarrassing reports of ghosts and phantoms.

A thin brown-skinned man, bedecked in silken Moorish garb that harkened to another millennium, approached them and bowed deeply. The man's scimitar glinted as if recently polished, but hung from his belt for purely decorative purposes. His moustache was thick, waxed and flowing, but his eyes were as dull and lifeless as pottery. Behind them raged no fire, no flicker of selfish desire or hopes. Or perhaps the Moroccans, too, had mastered the art of dispassion.

A good lot, Wilkes thought. They were fit and disciplined, tough and sinewy. Good fighters, for Arabs. He had seen them drive on into the reptilian sheen of European mechanized armies, swords and rifles flailing uselessly against the thickness of tanks and the storm of machine-gun fire. But they had driven on regardless. They had done so because their sultan had asked them to.

"My sultan desires to see you now," the man said tonelessly. He then swung open the heavy cedar doors and gestured the Englishmen through.

Within, the sultan of Morocco waited in his practised royal recline. He was careful to let the gold brocades be seen on the hem of his gown, and draped himself upon the sequined cushions with obvious intent. Like his ancestors, the sultan was true master over his domain, and it shone through in his attitude to the foreigners. He was dismissive towards them, rarely allowing excitement or surprise emotions he often felt while in their company! to be seen upon his noble visage. They came from a land of monarchs, too, he knew, and so held certain expectations of regal behaviour. He would satisfy those expectations, but also plant new ones.

Only the secure and the strong can afford to be supremely charitable in his regal manner, he had been told. So he revelled in shocking his guests with royal opulence and lavish eccentricities. His guests would want for nothing while sequestered in his realm, but they would serve to further educate him about the motivations of northern men.

Though a young man nearing forty, he preferred the image of elder sagacity, even proffering a greying beard and thoughtful demeanour unmatched with a childish intent. He would prod at the foreigners' egos, seek out the weaknesses he knew were there: envy and disdain, and the paradox of humility wrapped in haughtiness. He would tell them tales of excesses and triumphs, then of trying times and of the ancientness he knew they lacked. At times he would water the wine or undercook the meat, never to the point of rudeness, but only to measure their palates and resolve.

Across his hall he had draped silken banners and rich fabrics with which to impress the miserable Europeans. He knew them. He knew their hearts. They were strong in weapons, their nations rich in paper but poor in gold. They were filled with desires, fed with promises and compliments. As single men, they were devoid of measurable wealth, except for those men too fat to leave England. As a people, they had no mythology. And that's why they were destined to be misdirected, despite their lizard-like devices of strength and destruction.

Wilkes he understood best of all. He resembled one of Prince Faisal's "desert-loving English." Wilkes was like one of their women: sly, externally strong and defiant, but confused and easily moved. Like their women, Wilkes's poise compelled and intrigued him.

The sultan had once loved one of their women, many years ago. Her English birth name was a lost memory now, but he had renamed her Shahebina *instrument of God!* because Allah had sent her to open his eyes to the practices of the northern world.

Shahebina had flirted the way women always do, skirting that treacherous line between feline initiative and vulgar aggression. As always, though, it had been left to him to push flirtation to action, and their fires had finally mixed inside a royal tent alone in the cold desert night.

She was gone in a matter of days, attached to a medical mission. He had had many women before and since, but his body longed for hers. He had concluded that her beauty and exoticism, the strangeness of pink skin and an alien tongue, had captured his intrigue. There were others, however, who saw in this affair a more dire reading: that the sultan had seen the direction of the wind, and his sex had followed where his national pride refused to proceed.

Moroccan beauty was still untouchable, as was the poetic purity of Islamic love and courtship. The appeal of this pink woman, it spoke not to his thirsty eyes nor to the needs that beckoned from beneath his gowns, but to that shared ether of human experience that longs for connection between points of extreme distance. It was that same ether that is best perceived within the stark minimalism of desert twilight, when the moon is unseen and the stars begin to pierce into the racial unconscious.

Where cognizant thought failed him, his brain made rigorous recordings. There were impressions of ghostly desert winds slamming hard against the tent walls, choking musky odours and shortened steamy breaths. Two separate bodies joined at points, not mingling in the ways of Eastern love. Both strived for release and compliance, neither seeking the gratification of the other, sharing only in a shower of sweat.

On that night, too, they had seen something strange upon the sands, that thing born of scores of extinguished lives lain waste before the procession of history. It was a result, no doubt, of their bodies' shared ecstacy, and of the desert's power over minds. Yet it was like that wind, the sultan thought, that blows one's ship away from home but towards destiny. A vision upon the desert was not to be ignored, but the roles of all factors present must be assessed. And where did this pink woman fit in?

"Wilkes," the sultan said, waving them to their cushions alongside the silent noblemen and ministers. Wilkes nodded to his sergeant, and the latter held open a burlap sack. Wilkes stuck his hand in it, and pulled out a decayed human head.

"Marshall Hausen. Beheaded with one of your scimitars," Wilkes said. The sultan nodded appreciatively as Wilkes placed the grisly prize by his wine glass.

"The bounty will be sent to your platoon," the sultan said. The English, they fought for principle, their king, and their girlfriends. But the best of them could kill for money. They kill the Germans because the Germans wished to rape their principles, their king, and their girlfriends. Not a one would hesitate to plunge a dagger into an undefended German back. Yet they happily hunt boars with the German officers in their prisoner-of-war camps.

"Why do they do this?" the sultan's minister had asked at the time, when Wilkes had first requested permission for the boar hunt. The sultan's mouth had opened in response, but little had trickled from it. He had considered a thoughtful reply based upon his careful study of the English attitude, but instead, quite uncontrollably, his mind had ridden a hot wind back to that redolent evening with Shahebina.

"What is new, Wilkes?" he said.

"Your Highness," Wilkes said between mouthfuls of basted mutton, "we expect victory in Africa shortly."

"Then you will be missed."

"Thank you." Wilkes wasn't certain if the monarch's comment was one of genuine affection, mere politeness, or some kind of slight. But that wasn't his job, he convinced himself. "I miss Yorkshire very much, but I know I'll miss Rabat when my time comes, especially in light of Your Highness's great generosity to my men."

It was always the same: the soldiers who misinterpreted their military commission as diplomacy; the king who tired of administration. The course of dinner was set in jute woven by Greek muses, their conversation crafted by a poor bard. News from the battlefront was to be interspersed with comparisons of European and Islamic methods of war, art, dress, cookery, and love-making. The unseeing eyes of Marshall Hausen observed it all with resolute assiduity, his posthumous espionage career well under way.

Sometimes the sultan wished that one of them had true courage. With that sharpened temerity, a narrow path could be bored through the screens of dispassion, and their fires could be mixed in a different way. It was perverse, this intrigue with matters of little spiritual consequence. Basted mutton gratified their bodies, and in war they were bathed in a common sweat. With true courage, though, they could mingle and associate according to the pithy dictates of Eastern love.

"What's it like being a king?" Shahebina had asked, so long ago inside the tent. It was not an uncommon question. Many a bedmate had asked him that before. But their curiosity had focused on the vestments of power, the ability to dictate one's own destiny and the destinies of others. What the Englishwoman had wondered, he surmised, was how he felt about the responsibility.

He had not known what to say. Kingship was not a matter of choice, nor was soldiering. Neither did peasants and concubines have choices. Shahebina would have abhorred that answer, he was sure. The soldiers of Christ hack to serve their masters because it is what they want, not merely what they are expected to do.

And so another question was offered, one more cunning and subtle: "What, my sultan, do you think of the English?" She had been massaging his earlobes at the time, in the Eastern manner he had shown her. His diplomatic ways did not permit a true heartfelt response, even in that most tender of moments. She was, in her way, a representative of her people.

In the end, he had not been able to answer. His throat was choked with deep feeling, his tongue swollen with sexual abundance. The strange thing upon the desert had followed soon after, but it was altogether unimportant. Shahebina's image was so clear now, almost real, strengthened by the presence of similarly clever and sentient English. In a cruel play of light and divine spectra, her face slowly melted away to be replaced by the rakishly hard features of Lieutenant Wilkes.

"There is another matter, Your Highness," Wilkes said. "Some of the men have seen a . . . thing . . . in the desert at night. A spirit, they say . . ."

"Say no more," the sultan said. "It's a trick of the light when the moon is new. That's all." The dinner came to an end, and the sultan retired to his chambers, leaving his ministers to bid farewell to the Englishmen.

Perhaps if that true courage had been found he would have allowed himself to discuss the strange thing in the desert. But it was for Moroccans, not English, like an intimacy not shared between lovers. It was known that beneath the illusory glare of the absent new moon, a silvery four-legged apparition was sometimes seen to sail across the frigid desert. Its fiery mane drew corsairs of dust, its tail that of a questionable comet: subtle, not thunderous.

From where it came, no one could substantiate. Its origins were thickly shrouded in history. Even more obscure was its destination. At a point, some observers of unshakeable conviction once reported, it exploded into ten thousand and one paler beasts, each galloping in a different direction. At times, these smaller beasts would glance back, as if beckoning observers to follow into uncertain futures. None was seen to cease bounding, but all were seen to flicker from existence, much like a dim star drowned by impending daylight.

Whether delusion or apparition, the thing had emerged from the sublime ether of shared human experience, a domain of delight, confusion, and terror best perceived upon the sensory desert. In which direction the beasts would recoalesce, he could not know, except that he the king had unerringly followed the phantoms that had galloped northward. Upon this reflection, the saddened sultan looked to the back of the departing lieutenant Wilkes and wondered anew if Shahebina even remembered her adopted Arabic name.

Seasonal Youth

IT WAS a normal day, not too hot, not too cold, no excess of chores or of idleness. Yes, the day was ideal. The warm sun glowed brightly over the gently curving horizon. The scene was pretty, colourful and, again, quite normal.

Down past the streams, the village slept quietly, and all the inhabitants were off working in the fields. It was a good day for such work, for the air was charged with invigorating currents, and the sky was that peculiar hue of rural happiness. It was such a good day, in fact, that one would not wish it ever to end. And so it was with Bol.

It was good to be young, Bol thought, because youth is the only reason for living. Saplings spring forth in early summer; and even the first cold hints of winter spell youthful wonder for the children of the village.

Bol turned his attention to the waning hillside, so green and vibrant. This was how life was meant to be lived. It would be a pity to waste your years chasing dreams, he thought, when you could enjoy your entire existence right here in your own village, where adventures were to be found in every anthill, romance behind every barn.

Up ahead he saw a tattered figure: an old man, no doubt, come to beg from the farmers. Very well then, Bol thought, I shall give him some of my fruit. He set his sack down upon the soft earth and began searching for a suitable morsel.

As he looked up again, he saw the old beggar only a few feet from him, but the vagrant took no notice of the youth, only of his own shoes; and he was muttering under his breath.

Bol stood upright and held his hand out in front of him (in it was a gloriously red apple). But the transient failed to notice his offer, and kept on walking right past Bol and his gift!

"Well that's no way to treat a fellow traveller!" said Bol to himself and he sidled up alongside the strange individual. He began to speak but stopped in midsentence, for he caught a wisp of what the stranger was muttering: "Three hundred and eight, three hundred and nine, three hundred and ten . . ."

Good grief, Bol thought, he's counting to himself!

"Excuse me, good sir," said Bol. "Excuse me!"

"Eh? What? Who are you?" The stranger looked rather startled.

"I am Bol. I live down at that village." Bol pointed behind him.

"So, I see. Well, what do you want . . . Bol?"

"I see that you are hungry. May I offer you some food?" He held the apple up to the stranger's face.

"N-no thank you, son. I have work to do."

Now this was quite a surprise to young Bol who had always considered work to be digging, cleaning, harvesting, or some activity of comparable sweat production.

"Pardon me, good sir," he asked, "but what kind of work are you involved in?"

"What kind of work?! Why, you must be young, indeed!" The vagrant brightened some. "I am counting. I count every step I take."

"But why?" Bol was now thoroughly bewildered.

"To see how far I've been, of course! Here, you try it."

Bol hung his head low and mumbled apologetically. "I'm sorry," he said. "I'm not allowed to stray far from home."

"No problem," the beggar said, "Just you walk about in wide circles around the hill."

No harm in trying, Bol said inwardly. He began to take careful steps around the green hillock, never removing his eyes from his stained and hardened shoes. Twelve, thirteen, fourteen . . . ninety-six, ninety-seven . . .

Bol yawned most profusely. He looked into the sky and stretched his aching muscles. He reached into his sack for a snack but found only rotten fruit.

And the stranger was gone. Now that was mighty queer.

But the queerest thing of all was that Bol could not find his beloved village. No matter how long or hard he searched, the village could not be seen through the wailing blizzard.

And Bol felt old, very old.

Camel's Lips

"WHAT'S THE colour of sadness?" I was asked once over a warm beer. "Or, for that matter, what's the texture of anger?" They were words plucked from a bad '60s song or a pretentious lit-mag.

The asker herself was a renegade from Tom Jones, cast in wicker and tempered by experience. The questions ran together as if on a production line, hued in the colours of brevity and desperation. "Have you ever caressed the lips of a camel?" she asked in all seriousness.

Shamefully, I confessed that I had not, but that I had nudged with my knees the backs of an elephant's ears ... "No," she said. "It's not the same thing." She was enchanted by texture, my demonic little camel rubber. Macho tales of jungle conquest on elephant back would not suffice.

The howls of wicked February slammed hard against the windows then; we could not know of the comfortable spring morning that lay in wait. And as I squinted at her, hoping to see the backs of her eyes through a haze of alcoholic fuzziness, a window blind was thrown open suddenly, washing her pixie face in the intense beam of the streetlight across the road.

On her smooth face, shadows danced, in a Javanese ballet, a staccato *Ramayana,* an allegorical tale of romance and wickedness played out in the valleys between her nose and upper lip, and between her left bottom eyelid and cheekbone.

Listen: it was like watching insects feast on lifeless carrion, but this corpse was animate. Pale she was, and English, too, but there was a warmth and maybe fire simmering inside that grinning head.

"What's my tongue taste like?" I said, then planted my lips against hers, quite suddenly; some would say violently.

"Like semen," she said, and almost giggled. I made a face and pretended to spit. But the thought was erotic, it was.

I took her by the hand and we danced down the stairs and through the waiting restaurant orifice. From a warm fluid plenitude we crossed into the desert of dying winter, our beer-filled bellies sloshing like fat in a dromedary's hump.

Beneath that musical streetlight, I kissed her once more, and let my right hand drift to her cooling lips.

And I caressed them.

I had read of creatures like her: seductive pixies, sirens, waifish nymphs who beckon in partial dress, always appealing to the animal in men. But for me the attraction was not her body, it was in the odd sentences that would erupt unannounced from between her precious lips.

"You know," she said, as we made our way arm-in-arm across the desert of snow to my waiting apartment. "I always found Watson more interesting than Holmes."

I tried to match pace: "I always felt Watson was the kind of man who must constantly inspect his zipper to make sure it's not undone. Very unsettling."

"Oh no. Watson was the sort of fellow who could bring most women, and the occasional man, to such heightened orgasmic ecstacy that soon afterward she must melt into a pool of tears, dismayed profoundly that such sexual bliss would be forevennore unattainable."

I paused and looked at her. Such unrehearsed splendour of word! Such spoken allures could not be matched by any mere feature of flesh, nor by any provocative scent nor wet sexual embrace. And I had to question their spontaneity. As if to a siren's song, had I sailed willingly into an inescapable, designed demise?

We flowed into my home, almost melting into each other now that artificial heat sapped the cold from our faces. Our ears were caressed by the subconscious static of my dying television, and the contours of her face seemed to flush in response to the unobtrusive sound. I inspected those facial valleys intimately now, exploring the grooves and pores with tongue and eyelash. Her rough and bitter tongue snaked inside my mouth, and I was a bit surprised to find that it was not, after all, forked! But blunt and relentless, it probed my palate, the flatness from which fricatives, glottal stops and other wonders of linguistic artistry would normally issue.

She withdrew, suddenly, to speak of further inanities and nonsequiturs. "If you were to kiss a camel, would it taste of the desert?" and "To make love on the desert sands-would it be as enjoyable as on the wet sands of a beach?" And I considered the sensation of hot rivers of sand flowing through the crevices of my body, becoming lodged between the grindings of our intertwined limbs, and coated and cooled by the fluids of ardour.

We continued on until daybreak, rising from our feast only briefly at times to sniff the winter air that crept through the cracks in my window, and to add randomly to the uncertain and nonlinear sentences that dribbled from the ignored television.

On that screen, I saw at last as I separated myself from my sleeping siren, was a black-and-white woman as sultry as that which lay next to me. She plucked a filter-tipped cigarette from her Hollywood mouth and began to speak. But a man put a finger to her lips, silencing her, and bent close to kiss her with his droopy, dry camel's lips.

Son of Caine

THE SINGAPORE School For Boys brandished pillarlike teeth of cement and classical arched orifices that gaped and craned to devour poor learned Mr Hussein as he approached its mouth with fear.

That was on first arrival, a day of great stellar import and auspicious happenings. On that day a traditional lion dance had progressed down Bencoolen street, only to be tragically dispersed by a runaway truck; and the culture minister had erected a symbolic obelisk for commercial good fortune, then had watched it plummet through the ceiling of the shopping mall to which it was supposed to bring luck.

Being a physics teacher, and therefore not one for such superstitious nonsense, Mr Hussein had summoned ethereal courage and had boldly proceeded through the toothy maw into the cement box which housed the best, the brightest and the wealthiest sons of the British families who had chosen to remain long after Independence. Leaving behind the swarming shadows of vultures and the occasional scurrying black cat, he marched down the building's throat, sucking back the flood of lard that threatened to burst over his tightened belt, and desperately gripping his heavy briefcase with the weak and trembling stubby fingers of his left hand.

Corridors that glowed awkwardly, like the aura of flickering torches in an anachronistic Jules Verne novel, throbbed with membranous regularity as the chitter of childish argument soaked through to his dishy ears in waves and torrents. A tall figure clad in a sleek black suit stepped out from a thyroid-shaped office, the figure's black skin and curly black hair surreal in the imagined firelight. With a long powerful arm extended, it spoke in a commanding puissant baritone: "You must be the Paki."

Mr Hussein had never been adept at witty banter, or at countering statements that others might construe as slights. Certainly, within, he waged the war of the thoughtful: considering appropriate miens and attitudes, responses and rebuttals. A familiar but unpleasant taste formed in his slitted mouth; foulness of tongue incensed a repugnant imagined smell, and soon even the bowels quaked. His proud heart prepared retort upon rejoinder, but the best he could manage was a limp handshake and a perfected vacant expression.

"I am Oki Akibe, the Headmaster," the African said. "You may call me Headmaster Akibe, Mr Headmaster, Mr Akibe or just Sir. I suggest you demand the same of your students. With you here, there's three of us to run this place. Though, I admit, one man is all you need to handle these little English faggots."

Perhaps impressed by the ferocious beauty of the feral Headmaster Akibe, Mr Hussein maintained his patented empty countenance and allowed himself to be led to a windowed door. Through it he saw a class in session history, it seemed taught by a small-boned middle-aged bespectacled white man whose unchanging smile may have been surgically included.

"Horace Whitby," Akibe said. "Royal wimp of Her Majesty's educational college. Makes the faggots so jittery I have to sedate them when they come into my class."

Mr Hussein stared incredulously. "Know how to deal with the worst ones?" Akibe's was a rhetorical question, no doubt. "You poke 'em in the rib with your thumbnail!" He inserted a well-worn and practised thumbnail above his new colleague's bottom floating rib. The little Pakistani almost embedded his toenails in the ceiling.

As the days progressed, it was clear that three teachers were one too many for barely forty students. Indeed, Mr Hussein began to feel like Philoctotes of the Argonauts, or the fourth Stooge, the fifth wheel, or the little piggy who ran whee whee whee all the way home. That is, until a rather odd thing happened to noiseless Horace Whitby.

Not being a talkative soul, Mr Hussein had had ample opportunity to absorb shards from the rumour wheel. Gleaned from crude declarations by the older boys, shadowy side sentences spewed out from the secretarial crew, and blatant assertions courtesy of Headmaster Akibe, it was known that Horace Whitby's favourite masturbatory perversion involved surgical gloves and a global relief map. It further emerged that Whitby sometimes enjoyed the participation of some of the senior students in these questionable geographic activities.

As these allegations became accepted as truth, it was not altogether surprising when Horace Whitby, adorned solely with sunglasses and illusory might, soared like a buzzard from the headpiece of the school's topmost balustrade and came crashing to a most final death.

A tragedy, to be sure, but one whose benefits were not entirely invisible to the craftier portion of Mr Hussein's otherwise docile persona. He was able to assimilate Whitby's classes so that he was now teaching the previously unheard of subject called "Literature of Historical Physics." And with this new responsibility came a larger classroom, higher wages, and a position further down the oesophagus of the Singapore School For Boys.

Often having considered himself one of Rushdie's "translated men," offering "stereoscopic vision" in place of "world sight," Mr Hussein felt born into the position that now beckoned him: that of the Islamic teacher to Old Empire white boys on the tetracultured isle of Singapore.

It was about time, he told himself. After all, he had just recently made the all-important transition from September-to-August weekly agendas to January-to-December full daily planners. And so he set forth with a passion, or rather a demonstrated competence, for his new class, injecting Rushdie and Mukherjee, Lao Tse and the Koran wherever he could.

Perhaps his was an ideal example of the dichotomous anomaly of a square-peg mind-set forced into a circular body. Convinced beyond reasonable question that his was the new multi-integrated neo-Renaissance high-charisma global educational approach, his persona was yet unable to translate such proper paragons through the somewhat limited capacities of his vocal and physical apparatus. In short, Mr Hussein was not seen as a dynamic individual.

But he was entirely unaware of his image. That is, until he discovered a mischievous little rhyme carved into the underside of a chalkboard eraser in his classroom. It read:

Oblivious to light, oblivious to rain,

Oblivious to insults, slights and pain,

He's faster than a snail, but slower than a train.

He thinks he's Tarzan, but we call him Jane.

Not quite a Christian, though a son of Caine,

He's trite, not patrician, our Mr Hussein.

He had thought the culprit to be Alfred, the poet prodigy who had memorized Joyce's *Ulysses* at age ten. In truth, it had been Otto Nobbles, the nerdy stuttering little boy who had previously displayed no obvious marketable talent other than an uncanny ability to insert a whole index finger to the third knuckle! into his gaping nostril.

On the morning on which he prepared to confront Alfred with the atrocity, further unusual circumstances seemed to upset the astrological balance of things. A Hawaiian fire dancer had accidentally set ablaze the roast pig at Raffles Hotel; a national noodle-eating contest had ended abruptly with much vomit and at least one case of appendicitis; and the culture minister had had the great misfortune to be inspecting the tracks of the island's famed train station when someone inside a train caboose flushed a toilet.

Certainly, even Mr Hussein noticed that something astrological was afoot, because he needed two and a half cups of calming Sri Lankan tea to successfully complete the proper Windsor knotting of the morning necktie. But, upon victorious completion of this task and the regular ablutions, he advanced unto the stomach of the schoolhouse. His head swam somewhat from an unusual dream the night before: ambivalent impressions of a personal psychoanalysis, presided over by Freud and Rushdie, that had ended with a diagnosis of schizophrenia and general wimpiness.

"Mornin', wimpy little Paki," Headmaster Akibe chuckled as he shuffled into his thyroid office, cup of coffee in hand. The Windsor-knotted tie reflected with old school dignity in the imagined torchlight of the corridor. Mr Hussein countered the affront with his licensed vacant look, then proceeded into his classroom to deal with Alfred.

The teenage bard, bursting with self, reclined godlike in the uncomfortable pupil seat. No doubt aware of Otto Nobble's pathetic little rhyme, Alfred was prepared to imbibe the blame. Indeed, he salivated at the prospect. Tired of global relief maps and sore ribs, he was eager to feast his adolescent wit's fangs on this soft fat morsel that dared call itself a teacher.

Mr Hussein carefully placed his briefcase atop his desk, slowed for the roll of blubber that prevented a full bend, then searched for the right words with which to confront Alfred. The boy was remarkably attractive, Mr Hussein noticed then; lips red as Indian mud, eyes dark as Oliver Cromwell's soul, lines of an angelic face that joined exactly two centimetres below a pouting bottom lip at a soft and smoothly rounded apex called a chin. He was clad in rough black leather that failed to conceal the mandatory school tie and dress pants, but helped to accent the practised Apollonian recline.

"Do you know what your problem is?" Alfred asked suddenly, just as the visual survey neared its end. "Do you know why someone as smart as yourself is stuck in the large intestine of this shitty little schoolhouse? You're essentially a good man, Mr Hussein. You have an academician's mind, a poet's heart, the body of, uh, an opera singer, but the soul of a frightened child."

The blood drained from Mr Hussein's face.

"Your mind protects your soul, and both hold back your heart."

Such biting words that erupted from the underdeveloped mouth of a pampered little English faggot! The consumption of such typical fare as Joyce taught him could make him draw such rash conclusions! Yet the words stung with familiarity, as if their gist had been spoken to him before, perhaps in a dream. The stout little Pakistani trembled and threatened to sputter inwardly. On the outside was the trademark countenance of vacuity.

"Turn to page 126 and begin reading to yourselves," he said evenly. "I shall return shortly." He turned in slow motion, forcing one heavy foot to follow the other as he undertook the long voyage to the door. He was unsure where his heart was taking him, but his opera singer's body moved purposefully down the throbbing corridors.

He found himself in the atrium, the thyroid-shaped office occupied by the obnoxious Headmaster. His soul quaked with fear while his mind considered the possibilities. His heart and body forged on unhesitatingly, turning knobs, scanning rooms, recognizing faces and moving about.

"Hey! Hussein!" Akibe said. "Little Paki, shouldn't you be in class?"

"Hey! Akibe!" Mr Hussein said. "Shouldn't you have some class?" And he shoved the nail of his right thumb, as hard as he could, in between the African's eighth and ninth ribs.

Memories of that first day, though not so long ago, seemed so distant now. Ingestion of the Complete Rushdie had prepared him for much, but it had been the little Joycean disciple who had finally compelled action. Vague impressions of a beet-red African in midflight, an organic shudder that rippled down his sagging skin, and of a fecal bolus that swam in the saliva bath of his mouth, only to be shat out with violence, fought with the unsettled stars for mastery of a portly Pakistani persona.

His heart had relinquished control back to his soul, which seemed much denuded in many ways, but still hungered for some degree of safety and security. It was his body that displayed the lasting scars of adventure, though. As he sat rubbing his ass, having been thrown upon it, Mr Hussein looked back to the schoolhouse anus through which he had so recently flown and remarked that it was newly defanged and really quite harmless.

Sanjay and Allison

SOMETHING HIT Sanjay when Allison first walked into the room. Nothing actually touched his little body, but it jerked and reeled as if a baseball bat had been taken to the back of his neck.

At that moment, basking in the glow of his ripe seven-year-old's idealism, he became a believer in love-at-first-sight. His entire awareness, focused perhaps for the first time in his brief life, was drawn to Allison's fair form. She had floated in, on this last day of classes, bedecked in an atypical flowing gown. Her blonde hair bobbed coyly by her ears, her delicate features concealing the rambunctious tomboy skulking within.

So it was with a new sensation, that of profound unseen disappointment for no visible reason that Sanjay found himself in summer vacation. Normally a happy time of pointless play and mindless dithering, the warmest season saw his many thoughts wander elsewhere.

Something was different. In his belly, like the egg of an unseen and unfelt creature, a thing took hold and began to grow.

How horrifying it was to discover the unseen monster within himself. It was a lurking, slime-ridden beast that would be despised and shunned by other children because it, in its irrational monstrous way, longed to return to school. And school was uncool.

He remembered past summers spent frying ants with a magnifying glass, or skirting pedestrian traffic easily on his daredevil's tricycle. Those summers flitted by unnoticed and were quickly mourned as the first leaves of autumn touched pavement.

This time, however, the searing July afternoons were endless. For each agonizing day left to endure was a day without . . . what? He knew. He must have known.

He still joined the other boys in insulting the larger but sillier sex. What use were they? Yet one evening he found himself alone by the screen door that faced westward through his backyard. Way off in the distance invisibly so, in truth was the closed school. He was bewitched by the memory of beauteous precision cloaked in white lace.

Soon followed the three-wheeled dream quests into the treacherous western neighbourhoods; the dodging of crude preteen thugs who glided upon dull orange skateboards; the race across the unnamed cul-de-sac, chased by monstrous canines with teeth long as daggers; the inspirational glide down the death-defying slope of Withrow Road, all so he could finish his romantic journey in the fabled crescent called Thornecliffe, rumoured home of the divine Allison.

Monotonously, the days of summer dragged on. June flowed into July into August. Finally, autumn returned, and Grade Two beckoned.

On that first day back, Sanjay had bedecked himself (or had had his mother do so for him) in opulent regalia: his best plaid polyester suit, the height of 1974 chic for seven-year-olds.

Gnomelike in his austerity, he radiated great charm and allure, taking every opportunity to insult or abuse the apple of his eye. It was, of course, the day's accepted manner of courtship.

And Allison proved equally adept at hurling back the insults of affection. It was a beautiful thing.

The days passed quickly, as did the years. From the barrage of abuse grew a quiet friendship resembling a marriage, but no such thoughts were ever shared. Within his growing heart, Sanjay felt the complacent stings of isolated desire; learned to need them and like them.

He watched as Allison grew into a comely waifish teen, mistress of the realms of hormonal intrigue, while he remained the unspeaking dwarf, tied to his books and his secret thoughts.

He watched as she embraced the athletes, boys who smelled as men and strutted like bulls. He, meantime, mastered the unpopular arts of chess and mathematics, passports to seclusion. On his lips, he wore a smile for the portents of worldly knowledge that warmed his innards. Behind his glinting spectacles shone a distracted demeanour, a wandering eye for the Nordic beauty who sometimes passed before him.

He watched as she wove sudden and complex paths through unfathomable social circles, sometimes finding great pleasure and sometimes great pain, but always knowledge of a different kind. In his books were scribbled drawings of an angled face and bobbed hair, quatrains to repression and introspection.

He was not watching when she disappeared, another face that no longer materialized in the stream of one's passage. He had ceased to think of the real Allison, preferring instead his drawings and memories. That she was elsewhere, no longer in his realm, mattered little.

So when the years passed, and that circuitous path redoubled upon itself, he found he had not missed her all that much. Her reappearance was rather uneventful, but pleasant nonetheless.

He was a grown man now, no longer gnomelike but vaguely handsome, carried by a proud continence and deliciously probing eyes.

She was as comely as ever, though not the intimidating ingenou of her extreme youth.

"You know, Allison," Sanjay said smoothly. "I used to have the sorriest crush on you."

She grinned coyly, hoping to blush. "I know," she said.

In Flight

KAMLA BEGUM was not a tall woman but being straight-backed and queenly, she often convinced observers otherwise. Such an illusion was not possible, though, when she was hunched behind the wheel of a tops-down MG, hurtling down the highway like a banshee on speed.

What had mother said? *Come na, bibi, we go all stand like Cyclops when kingdom come.* Or something like that. Ma was always blabbering on about something, from haemorrhoids to the Archangel Azrael, something to incense great flapping of arms and splatterings of saliva.

The MG slipped along the roadway, much like a greased bullet through a gun's barrel; or like a sheathed penis along the vaginal canal; or anal canal mustn't be knocking alternative lifestyles, now.

Kamla had driven now four and two-thirds hours, away from the city, refusing even to glance at the fuel gauge. *When it dies, it dies!* That was the way, the path. No more always-looking-to-the-future-'cause-with-no-future-what-you-got?

Time to play the game, roll the dice, take your best shot, roll with the punches, don't you know.

Her bonnet, wrapped haphazardly but oh-so-sexily about her chocolate neck, fluttered in the wind. One little edge, white-laced softness adorned with golden tassels, persistently struck her left cheek.

Oh so annoying.

Tap tap tap. It's amazing how slight physical sensations can trigger useless memories. A toothbrush slips off a shining ivory tooth and collides into the tender inside wall of a little girl's cheek. A tent is blown away by ghostly forest winds, and the gentle rain drums softly on the side of its sleeping inhabitant's face. Tap tap.

Jehangir's voice, strangely feminine despite his steely thigh hairs, and the manly muscles of his lower abdomen: "You don't have to do this if you don't want to . . ." But she had taken him in her mouth, unaffected.

Tap tap tap.

She pressed harder on the accelerator, wishing that the MG had a manual transmission, and not an old lady's automatic. Her right hand jerked like a headless turkey, grasping hopelessly for a stick shift: a kind of automotive penis envy.

She felt that her heels were dragging along the pavement as in a *Flintstones* cartoon. She hit the brakes instead, instinctively. And the car ground to a halt.

Her head snapped back violently, thudding dully against the headrest. Whiplash. That's what people always have in car accidents, right? She massaged the back of her neck, hoping to incite some pain, but failed. *One good lawsuit, bibi, and we got plenty money for doctorin' school.* Pa wasn't a lawyer, but he certainly had the necessary lack of integrity to have made a fine one. Even if she had whiplash, whom could she sue? The Ministry of Transportation? *Baapur* !

There was smoke coming out of somewhere. She flowed out of the MG and began the walk to the nearest service station.

Won't that sissy-boy Jehangir be surprised, na? to find his precious oedometer rolled forward a couple million miles. Won't his oh-so-proper and tight progenitors be blasted away into the realm of the irretrievably shocked; won't Ma and Pa suck their chocolate thumbs and count their darling pennies when the lawyers' bills and bail bond fall on their doorstep, na? And won't the whole suckly brown gaggle shake their flabby jowls and mumble in shame when Kamla-bibi was finally seen exploding down the parkway on a Harley, clutching a black boy's muscular love handles.

All she had to do was find a cooperative black boy. And a motorcycle.

They were all disappointments, every last one. Towing the bloody line, they were; playin' the game; repeatin' the words; fulfilling the fucking roles. Even Jehangir, a jello-spined lower tetrapod cloaked in a handsome man's evil smile, had ended up being one of them. His only original thoughts involved things to do with his pecker.

Even the service station was a disappointment. Too many neon signs and "fine family dining establishments." Where was the broken-down washroom, the rickety old-timer on the rocking chair, the boarded-up general store run by the inbred banjo-plucking retard? *Life's not a film, bibi.* No, Pa, but it's not supposed to be a bloody sitcom either, right?

"Your life's a Virginia Woolf novel," Jehangir once said. "Except that that old faggot Quentin Crisp is playing the lead role!" *Slap!* Jehangir could be a real shit sometimes. Thank God this was Canada, where a girl didn't have to marry some foul-mouthed self-important know-it-all just because her parents liked him; just because he had a future. Thank God she was well within her rights to drive to nowhere, far as she wanted, far from hairy peckers and doctorin' school, and nobody would judge her for it.

Thank God.

"Can I help you?"

"Car trouble," she said. "Back eastward, less than a mile." She sized him up good: young, scruffy, muscular. Not too bright, but willing to please. And not black, either, but the next best thing: white. There was something about the greasy coveralls, the subtle odour of tobacco smoke mixed with grease . . . Reminded her of a Benetton ad, but this was no Marky Mark. This guy probably couldn't even spell "Mark." Then again, could Marky?

"I guess I could take a look," he said, scratching his unwashed head. Some kind of impeded thought process seemed to be taking place, hindered, no doubt, by the intrusion of various hair-consuming parasites into his cerebral cortex. "Okay, let's go."

"Walk?" Kamla asked.

"Yeah," he said. "Not far, right? You want I should take the pickup?"

She shook her head and sighed inwardly. No motorcycle. And beneath the neon glare of the Tim Horton's sign, she saw more clearly that he was, indeed, considerably less than Marky Mark. Where were the Springsteen videos of the world? Where were the unfound flowers cloaked in mechanics' garb, the unjudging grateful princes cast unto poverty by the inequities of global economics and biased monetary policy?

They walked, wordlessly. The occasional ruffled pant leg would brush up against Kamla's bare flesh, and she would once more see "Markisms" in her rescuer, perhaps roused by those uncontrollable spurts of event-provoked memories.

Got to break loose now, Kam, the pecker had said. *Got to do it all before medical school, you know.* Why? she had asked him, the prick. Because there's no life after school? *'Cause when we're married, you can't go 'round ogling boys in nightclubs.* But I don't like ogling boys in nightclubs, *you prick*. Then he had wanted to *do it* right there by the side of the highway. Maybe it was he who liked ogling boys in nightclubs, eh?

"You just snapped this doodad," the mechanic said, or something like that. He was bent over the MG, left leg crooked in a knowing stance. She surveyed his worker's body, defined even through the coveralls. She pictured his love handles, lithely muscled yet soft and curved the way they should be. The vision was in sharp contrast to Jehangir's gruff yet brittle form.

He pulled something out of the engine, then replaced it with something else. "She'll run now." He was smiling and sweaty, focused and almost alert, as if that painstaking thought process begun earlier had finally completed its course.

"Thanks," Kamla said, then muttered some indistinct offer of payment.

"No charge. Really." He handed her a petite cardboard rectangle. *A business card!* Roy Hawking, Mechanic. On the back was scribbled his phone number. "You look like the kinda girl who can appreciate a hog . . ."

"Excuse me?"

"A motorcycle?" His countenance, for a brief moment, returned to its original state of vacuity. "I got a Suzuki. Gimme a call, we go ridin'. Right?" His hands were forward, emulating the driving position on a cycle, and his lips were on the verge of making motorcycle sounds.

"Sure," Kamla said. She climbed into the MG and waved goodbye to Roy Hawking. She watched him walk off lazily, not a rushed cell in his being; certainly no hurried thought in his head. And she turned the car around, and headed back towards the city.

While I Drink My Moccacino

A BLACK woman with blonde hair, that cute but annoying California dumb-girl accent and a pink-faced skinny white boy on her arm it's all difficult to swallow.

Yet there she is, choosing her dessert at the counter while I stir whipped cream into my moccacino.

"Is she really black?" I ask myself. "Or just really well tanned?" As a brown man who walks, talks, dresses and eats like any hockey-playing gin-drinking cottage-owning sunburn-afflicted Euro-guy, this should not be an issue for me.

But I am forced to recall a scene from a favourite movie in which an Indian grandmother, distressed that her granddaughter is sleeping with a black man, says: "It's not colour. It's culture."

So the black girl lounging about the dessert counter giggles some more and mutters something about skiing near Zurich. From her mouth do not drip vulgar *hip-hop*-isms, nor any affected Jamaican bravado that even we most earnest stereotype-evaders might have come to expect.

The things that would have made her a threat or an annoyance a target for mall cops, talk-show hosts and social workers have been removed or replaced. All that is left of her blackness is the black itself: a quaintness.

I pay for my moccacino and leave a generous tip. Can't wait to get away to the cottage, catch a hockey game, play my easy-listening music, and vote conservative. Genetic urges for curry, drums, and cricket have never been a part of me.

So I wonder what it is that has compromised my culture, and that of this blonde black woman. And I finger the bountiful change, the glorious bills, in my pocket.

Motherland

SOMETIMES I feel that I once had a twin but he died in the womb, and nobody knew. It's a secret that only I contain, because only I ever saw him. I looked into his semiformed eyes through my own imperfect windows, and I knew there was a spiritual warmth between us, though our brains were still protoplasmic sludge.

So an entire human life, no matter how brief, is recorded and vaguely remembered solely within the confines of my mind. It's a grave responsibility. How could my mother not have known? The technology wasn't available in the backwards little tropical country that was our home. There, all a mother knows is what comes out after hours of pushing.

I think I must have lingered back as long as I dared, searching for my twin brother, whom I named Raul, until the very last moment. That's why I came out feet first.

I'm told I was a sad little boy for the first weeks of my life.

When we moved to Canada on my second birthday, the brown soil of our motherland was abruptly replaced with cold white snow. And the warm brown people with cold white ones. Of course, what could I know? I was just a snotty little baby.

But babies are almost telepathic; they know how their parents feel. A stuttered heartbeat, a surge in blood pressure, a stiffness behind the neck all these things are read by the baby about the mother who holds it.

I could not know the specific reasons for the changes I sensed. I was probably able to gawk at the empty practised smile of the cover-girl stewardess. But I could not fathom her shock at encountering people unaccustomed to dining utensils.

We settled in Toronto-the-Good where everyone got along famously because its unstated intolerance was not famous. My parents worked at hard labouring jobs for twelve hours each day, slept for four uncomfortable hours, and fought for the remaining eight.

This I could not understand and found frightening. On television, parents worked in snug offices, took their children to the Grand Canyon on vacations, and never ever said unkind words to each other. Why could my parents not see that they were doing everything wrong? Me, I was Greg Brady, Keith Partridge, Spiderman and Neil Armstrong. I had all the answers because I wasn't burdened by the darkness of the unsophisticated Third World. I knew nothing of, and cared less for, the history and texture of my motherland. But I learned Canada from Cartier to Trudeau, and Britain from the Normans to the House of Windsor.

The classroom was a high tribunal of most inviolate ideals. Behind those closed doors, nobody cared who you were or from where you had come. In particular, mathematics was the great leveller. Numbers never asked whether you were familiar with cutlery, or in what kind of job your father worked. I was master over numbers; they danced at my command.

But where the school was a warm un-judging haven, the school yard was a vicious battleground. I would dread the daily treks from our humble house through the school yard and back again. The slurs screeched through the atmosphere like hungry eagles, talons dragging through my scented hair. They soon ceased to be shocking, becoming simply another part of an onerous existence. On occasion, the screaming eagles descended to violence, and the fear would return anew. But children are such resilient creatures.

It took time to realize that the focus of their hatred was the accursed brown sheathing that encased my little body. That I would have this skin was a grievous injustice. Did I not walk and talk and react like one of them? Had I not struggled to forget my embarrassing accent and adopt the local slang that allowed my voice to be drowned in a sea of conforming inflections?

I was convinced that this was Raul fighting through my foetal memories to magically alter the colour of my skin. Raul had lived his whole life in the motherland. Of course he felt more brown than white.

Sometimes I would hear his uneducated voice call to me in thick *patwa*. This would happen as I tried to fall asleep, my wheezing lungs straining against the dry Canadian air. I'm not exactly sure what he said, but I suspect he was asking me who I was. He no longer recognized me.

On those nights, my dream would be the same. It involved a realization that my real parents a wealthy white couple who vacationed at the Grand Canyon had been searching for me all these years. And when they found me, they unzipped my hated brown sheath, and I emerged in all my golden blond glory.

As I grew older and more able to appreciate the hard lives of my parents, the dreams faded, and I was abashed at ever having produced them. Raul's *patwa* caterwauling was drowned out, as well, by softly spoken words of bad poetry phrased aloud, as best I could, in the Queen's perfect English. With those crafted stanzas came an awareness of Elizabethan beauty, of things classical and romantic. I found myself drawn to images of Western comeliness; entranced by pink-skinned girls who thought my brown was a suntan. My sexual fantasies gravitated towards an insubstantial practised smile brandished by a cover-girl stewardess.

Ashamed still of the darkness of my form, and the humbleness of my origins, action on these romantic desires was to be delayed a number of years. It wasn't until Raul found his voice again that I was able to approach a white woman. "Brown can be beautiful," he intoned, or something like that.

I was pleased that he had returned. I had missed him. To a certain extent, I felt that I had roots once more, but not in any identifiable country. My parents refer to the motherland as "back home," but I don't even remember the place. Visitors from that faraway land straighten their shirts and adjust their accents when I enter the room, because I walk with the airs of a white man. Sometimes white men stop their activities and adjust their behaviour when I enter their environment because I look like a brown man. My roots aren't with either of these groups.

When I think of "back home," my visions are of swirling sweet prenatal fluids, a miasma through which a pair of semideveloped eyes can be made out. They appeal to me in their lifeless way, and I am unable to reach them because my feet are already protruding through into the cold world.

Acknowledgements

First edition, 1999:

The stories in this collection were written over a period of many years, exploring issues that were relevant to me at different points in my life: racism, identity, immigration, family, and so on. The list of people to thank for their inspiration and support is therefore quite large.

Foremost is my immediate family who, despite the sarcastic flavour of our youth, never said a disparaging word about my untraditional endeavours, and were always interested and supportive: Walter, Sursati, Kalowatie, Abhi, Bhashkar and Phanindra. My clan is truly huge, and to list all the cousins, uncles and aunts who were also a positive influence would be a daunting task; but nevertheless I thank them, too.

There were many friends who contributed as unwitting editors and interim readers, never asking for recognition or acknowledgement: Melanie Stevenson, Linda Morra, Katie Sandusky, Sneh Aurora, Manjit Singh, Kalyani Kathiramalainathan, Sean McLoughlin, Marnie Johnston, Julia Lenardon, Tanya

Grout, Diamando Diamantakos, Mary Ellen Duff, Barbra Sniderman, Margaret Fong, Adam Stevens, Kristine O'Brien and Alexandra Schleicher. I also offer special thanks to Edmund Wong for taking a barrage of promotional photographs for me on his own time.

Lastly, genuine gratitude is extended to a handful of key players who appeared at various points in my professional writing career: Walton Chan, whose high school fan-zine offered me my first publication venue; Arvind Kumar who, as editor of India Currents magazine, gave me my first opportunity to write for a large magazine; and Nurjehan Aziz of TSAR Books for recognizing the value of Sweet Like Saltwater.

There were others, of course, whose influence was more subtle: teachers and friends to name but two groups. Perhaps I'll save them to acknowledge in future books!

Thank you all.

Second edition, 2015:

With the re-publication of *Sweet Like Saltwater* almost 16 years later, I'd like to reiterate my gratitude to Nurjehan Aziz for having allowed this collection to be shared with the world. With the 2015 edition, the only editorial change I have made is in the story, Far From Family. As was originally intended, mention of Suleyman's sword has been changed to Suleyman's word. This is in reference to the legend of King Suleyman having known a secret word that allowed him to control the djinns. This fact was unknown to the book s original editors, and it is therefore understandable that they corrected the reference in error.

I am proud that *Sweet Like Saltwater* has touched so many. These stories were very much a heartfelt personal expression of the most important existential questions of my youth, and it has given me an indescribable joy to have been approached by many readers, often young and of Caribbean extraction, who were moved by the book s resonating personal themes of migration and identity.

In 2000, *Sweet Like Saltwater* was awarded the Guyana Prize for Best First Work, and thus entered the literary history of the nation of my birth. It was a poetic moment of closure.

Author's Biography

First edition, 1999:

RAYWAT DEONANDAN is presently completing a Ph.D. in Epidemiology at the University of Western Ontario. A widely-published writer on a variety of topics, his short stories have appeared in six countries: Canada, the U.S.A., England, New Zealand, Japan and China (in translation). *Sweet Like Saltwater*

is his first book of fiction. He has been awarded two Hart House (University of Toronto) Literary Prizes, and took first prize in the 1995 Canadian Author's Association National Student Short Story Contest.

Widely travelled, Deonandan is interested in physical cultures, and has attained advanced standing in many Oriental martial arts, including a black belt in Shotokan karate. His other interests include public education, biotechnology, space exploration and ancient history.

Of Indian ancestry, Guyanese origin and Canadian citizenship, he considers Toronto his true home.

Second edition, 2015:

RAYWAT DEONANDAN is a professor with the Interdisciplinary School of Health Sciences at the University of Ottawa. He is a widely published and award-winning scientist, journalist, and novelist. His most recent non-fiction book is *Introduction To International Health Theory: An Interdisciplinary Perspective* (Kendall Hunt, 2014), and his most recent novel is *Divine Elemental* (TSAR Books, 2003). His personal website is www.deonandan.com.